For more than forty years,
Yearling has been the leading name
in classic and award-winning literature
for young readers.

Yearling books feature children's
favorite authors and characters,
providing dynamic stories of adventure,
humor, history, mystery, and fantasy.

Trust Yearling paperbacks to entertain,
inspire, and promote the love of reading
in all children.

OTHER YEARLING BOOKS YOU WILL ENJOY

THE WORRY WEB SITE, *Jacqueline Wilson*

BAD GIRLS, *Jacqueline Wilson*

VICKY ANGEL, *Jacqueline Wilson*

THE LOTTIE PROJECT, *Jacqueline Wilson*

DOUBLE ACT, *Jacqueline Wilson*

THE SUITCASE KID, *Jacqueline Wilson*

PICTURES OF HOLLIS WOODS, *Patricia Reilly Giff*

GRASS ANGEL, *Julie Schumacher*

WITH LOVE FROM SPAIN, MELANIE MARTIN
Carol Weston

The Story of Tracy Beaker

Jacqueline Wilson

Illustrations by
Nick Sharratt

A YEARLING BOOK

Published by Yearling, an imprint of Random House Children's Books
a division of Random House, Inc., New York

First American Edition 2001
First published in Great Britain by Doubleday, a division of the
Random House Group Ltd, in 1991

Visit us on the Web! www.randomhouse.com/kids

Educators and librarians, for a variety of teaching tools, visit us at
www.randomhouse.com/teachers

ISBN: 0-440-41807-0

Reprinted by arrangement with Delacorte Press

Printed in the United States of America

November 2002

10 9 8 7 6

To Bryony, David, Miranda, Jason and Ryan

MY BOOK ABOUT ME

ABOUT ME

My name is Tracy Beaker.

I am 10 **years** 2 **months old.**

My birthday is on May 8. It's not fair, because that dopey Peter Ingham has his birthday then too, so we just got the one cake between us. And we had to hold the knife to cut the cake together. Which meant we only had half a wish each. Wishing is for babies anyway. Wishes don't come true.

I was born at some hospital somewhere. I looked cute when I was a little baby but I bet I yelled a lot.

I am   inches tall. I don't know. I've tried measuring with a ruler but it keeps wobbling about and I can't reach properly. I don't want to get any of the other children to help me. This is my private book.

I weigh   pounds. I don't know that either. Jenny has a scale in her bathroom but it's in stones. I don't weigh many stones. I'm little and skinny.

My eyes are   black and I can make them go all wicked and witchy. I quite like the idea of being a witch. I'd make up all these incredibly evil spells and wave my wand and ZAP! Louise's golden curls would all fall out and ZAP! Peter Ingham's silly squeaky voice would get sillier and squeakier and he'd grow whiskers and a long tail and ZAP! . . . there's not room on this bit of the page, but I've still got all sorts of ZAPs inside my head.

My hair is   fair and very long and curly. I am telling fibs. It's dark and difficult and it sticks up in all the wrong places.

My skin is   full of pimples when I eat a lot of sweets.

Stick a photo of yourself here.

I'm not really cross-eyed. I was just making a silly face.

I started this book on I don't know. Who cares what the date is? You always have to put the date at school. I got fed up with this and put 2091 in my Day Book and wrote about all these rockets and spaceships and monsters zooming down from Mars to eat us all up, as if we'd all whizzed one hundred years into the future. Miss Brown got really annoyed.

MORE THINGS ABOUT ME

Things I like

My lucky number is 7. So why didn't some fantastic rich family make me their foster child when I was seven, then?

My favorite color is blood red, so watch out, ha-ha.

My best friend is Well, I've had lots and lots, but Louise has gone off with Justine and now I haven't got anyone just at the moment.

I like eating everything. I like birthday cake best. And any other kind of cake. And Smarties and Mars bars and big buckets of popcorn and gummy spiders and Ben & Jerry's and Big Macs with french fries and strawberry milk shakes.

My favorite name is Camilla. There was a lovely little baby at this other home and that was her name. She was a really sweet kid with fantastic hair that I used to try to get into loads of little braids and it must have hurt her sometimes but she never cried. She really liked me, little Camilla. A family picked her to be their foster child quick as a wink. I begged her foster mom and dad to bring her back to 'see me but they never did.

I like drinking strong beer. That's a joke. I *have* had a sip of light beer once but I didn't like it.

My favorite game is playing with makeup. Louise and I once borrowed some from Adele, who's got tons. Louise was a bit boring and just tried to make herself look beautiful. I turned myself into an incredible vampire with evil shadowy eyes and blood dribbling down my chin. I really scared the little ones.

My favorite animal is Well, there's a rabbit called Lettuce at this home but it's a bit limp, like its name. It doesn't sit up and give you a friendly lick like a dog. I think I'd like a Rottweiler—and then all my enemies had better WATCH OUT!

My favorite TV program is horror movies.

Best of all I like   being with my mom.

Things I don't like

the name   Justine. Louise. Peter. Oh, there's heaps and heaps of names I can't stand.

eating   stew. Especially when it's got big fatty lumps in it. I used to have this horrid foster mother called Auntie Peggy and she was an awful cook. She used to make this slimy stew that looked like throw-up and we were supposed to eat it all up, every single bit. Yuck.

Most of all I hate   Justine. That Monster Gorilla. And not seeing my mom.

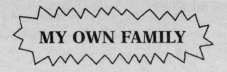

MY OWN FAMILY

Stick a photo of you and your family here.

This was when I was a baby. See, I was sweet then. And this is my mom. She's ever so pretty. I wish I looked more like her.

The people in my own family are My mom. I don't have a dad. I lived with my mom when I was little and we got on great but then she got this Monster Gorilla Boyfriend and I hated him and he hated me back and beat me up and so I had to be taken away to a children's home. No wonder my mom sent him packing.

My own family lives at   I'm not sure exactly where my mom lives now because she has to keep moving around because she gets fed up living in one place for long.

The phone number is   Well, I don't know, do I? Funny, though, I always used to take this toy telephone in the playhouse at school and pretend I was phoning my mom. I used to have these long, long conversations with her. They were just pretend, of course, but I was only about five then and sometimes they got to be quite real.

Things about my family that I like   I like my mom because she's pretty and good fun and she brings me lovely presents.

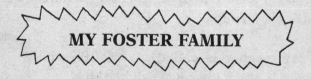

MY FOSTER FAMILY

There's no point filling this part in. I haven't got a foster family at the moment.

I've had two. There was Auntie Peggy and Uncle Sid first of all. I didn't like them much and I didn't get on with the other kids so I didn't care when they got rid of me. I was in a children's home for a while and then I had this other couple. Julie and Ted. They were young and friendly and they bought me a bike and I thought it was all going to be great and I went to live with them and I was ever so good and did everything they said and I thought I'd be staying with them until my mom came to get me for good but then . . . I don't want to write about it. It ended up with me getting thrown out THROUGH NO FAULT OF MY OWN. I was so mad I smashed up the bike so I don't even have that anymore. And now I'm in a new children's home and they've advertised me in the papers but there weren't many takers and now I think they're getting a bit desperate. I don't care, though. I expect my mom will come soon anyway.

MY SCHOOL

My school is called   It's Kinglea Junior School. I've been to three other schools already. This one's okay, I suppose.

My teacher is called   Ms. Brown. She gets angry if we just call her Miss.

Subjects I do   Story-writing. Arithmetic. Games. Art. All sorts of things. And we do Projects, only I never have the right stuff at the Home so I can't do it properly and get a star.

10

I like Story-writing best. I've written so many stories, and I do pictures for them too. I make some of them into books. I made Camilla a special baby book with big printed words and pictures of all the things she liked best, things like TEDDY BEAR and ICE CREAM and YOUR SPECIAL FRIEND TRACY.

I also like Art. We use poster paints. We've got them at the Home too but they get all grungy and messed up and the brushes are useless. They've got good ones at school. On the page before this, there's a painting I did yesterday. If I was a teacher I'd give it a gold star. *Two* gold stars.

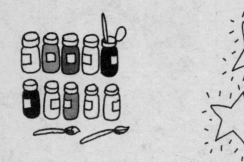

My class is 3a.

People in my class I can't list all their names, or I'd be here all night. I don't know some of them yet. There's not much point making friends because I expect to be moving on soon.

Other teachers Oh, they're all boring. Who wants to write about them?

I get to school by going in the minibus. That's how all the kids in the Home get to school. I'd sooner go in a proper car or walk it by myself but you're not allowed.

It takes hours minutes. It varies. Sometimes it takes ages because the little kids can't find their pencil cases and the big ones try to skip school and we just have to hang around waiting.

Things I don't like about school They all wear gray things—that's the uniform—and I've only got navy things from my last school. The teachers know why and I don't get into trouble but the other kids stare.

BEING IN FOSTER CARE

My social worker is called Elaine and sometimes she's an awful pain, ha-ha.

We talk about all sorts of boring things.

But I don't like talking about my mom. Not to Elaine. What I think about my mom is private.

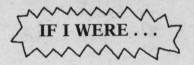

IF I WERE . . .

older, I would live in this really great modern house all on my own, and I'd have my own huge bedroom with all my own things, special bunk beds just for me so that I'd always get the top one and a Mickey Mouse alarm clock like Justine's and my own giant set of poster paints and I'd have some felt-tip pens as well and no one would ever get to borrow them and mess them up and I'd have my own television and choose exactly what programs I want, and I'd stay up till past twelve every night and I'd eat at McDonald's every single day and I'd have a

big fast car so I could whiz off and visit my mom whenever I wanted.

a policeman, I would arrest the Monster Gorilla and I'd lock him up in prison forever.

a kitten, I would grow very long claws and sharp teeth and scratch and bite everyone so they'd get really scared of me and do everything I say.

yelled at, I would yell back.

invisible, I would spy on people.

very tall, I would stamp on people with my great big feet.

very rich, I would buy my own house and then . . . I've already done that. I'm getting fed up writing all this. What's on the next page?

MY OWN STORY

Use this space to write your story.

THE STORY OF TRACY BEAKER

Once upon a time there was a little girl called Tracy Beaker. That sounds a bit stupid, like the start of a soppy fairy tale. I can't stand fairy tales. They're all the same. If you're very good and very beautiful with long golden curls, then, after you've swept up a few cinders or had a long nap in a cobwebby palace, this prince comes along and you live happily ever after. Which is fine if you happen to be a goody-goody and look gorgeous. But if you're bad and ugly then you've got no chance whatsoever. You get given a silly name like Rumpelstiltskin and nobody invites you to their party and no one's ever grateful even when you do them a great big favor. So of course you get a bit teed off with this sort of treatment. You stamp your feet in a rage and fall right through the floorboards or you scream yourself into a frenzy and you get locked up in a tower and they throw away the key.

I've done a bit of stamping and screaming in my time.

And I've been locked up heaps of times. Once they locked me up all day long. And all night. That was at the first Home, when I wouldn't settle down because I wanted my mom so much. I was just little then but they still locked me up. I'm not fibbing. Although I do have a tendency to tell a few fibs now and again. It's funny, Auntie Peggy used to call it Telling Fairy Tales.

I'd say something like "Guess what, Auntie Peggy, I just met my mom in the garden and she gave me a ride in her flashy new sports car and we went down to the shopping arcade and she bought me my very own huge bottle of perfume, that posh Poison one, just like the bottle Uncle Sid gave you for your birthday, and I was messing around with it, playing Murderers, and the bottle sort of tipped and it's gone all over me as I expect you've noticed, but it's my perfume, not yours. I don't know what's happened to yours. I think one of the other kids took it."

You know the sort of thing. I'd make it totally convincing, but Auntie Peggy wouldn't even really listen. She'd just shake her head at me and get all angry and red and say, "Oh, Tracy, you naughty girl, you're Telling Fairy Tales again." Then she'd give me a smack.

Foster mothers aren't supposed to smack you at all. I told Elaine that Auntie Peggy used to smack me and Elaine sighed and said, "Well, sometimes, Tracy, you really do ask for it." Which is a lie in itself. I have never in my life said, "Auntie Peggy, please will you give me a great big smack?" And her smacks really hurt too, right on the back of your leg where it stings most. I didn't like that Auntie Peggy at all. If I was in a real fairy tale I'd put a curse on her. What about a huge wart right on the end of her nose? Frogs and toads coming wriggling out of her mouth every time she tries to speak? No, I can make up better than that. She can have permanent great big boogers hanging out of her nose that won't go away no matter how many times she blows it, and whenever she tries to speak she'll make this terribly loud Rude Noise. Great! Oh dear. You can't win. Elaine, my stupid old social worker, was sitting beside me when I started writing THE STORY OF TRACY BEAKER and I got the giggles making up my brilliant curses for Auntie Peggy, and Elaine looked surprised and said, "What are you laughing at, Tracy?"

I said, "Mind your own business," and she said, "Now, Tracy," and then she looked at what I'd written, which is a bit rude, seeing as it's supposed to be

18

very private. She sighed when she got to the Auntie Peggy part and said, "Really, Tracy!" and I said, "Yes, really, Elaine." And she sighed again and her lips moved for a moment or two. That's her taking a deep breath and counting up to ten. Social workers are supposed to do that when a child is being difficult. Elaine ends up doing an awful lot of counting when she's with me.

When she got to ten she gave me this big false smile. Like this.

"Now look, Tracy," said Elaine. "This is your own special book about you, something that you're going to keep forever. You don't want to spoil it by writing all sorts of silly, smart-alecky, rude things in it, do you?"

I said, "It's my life and it hasn't been very special so far, has it, so why shouldn't I write any old rubbish?"

Then she sighed again, but sympathetically this time, and she put her arm around me and said,

"Hey, I know you've had a hard time, but *you're* very special. You know that, don't you?"

I shook my head and tried to wriggle away.

"Yes, you are, Tracy. Very very special," Elaine said, hanging on to me.

"Then if I'm so very very special how come no one wants me?" I said.

"Oh dear, I know it must have been very disappointing for you when your second placement went wrong, love, but you mustn't let it depress you too much. Sooner or later you'll find the perfect placement."

"A fantastic rich family?"

"Maybe a family. Or maybe a single person, if someone really suitable came along."

I gave her this long look. "You're single, Elaine. And I bet you're suitable. So why don't you foster me, eh? Then I could be your foster child."

It was her turn to wriggle then.

"Well, Tracy. You know how it is. I mean, I've got my job. I have to deal with lots of children."

"But if you fostered me you could stop bothering with all the others and just look after me. They give you money if you foster. I bet they'd give you lots extra because I'm difficult and I've got behavior problems and all that. How about it, Elaine? It would be fun, honest it would."

"I'm sure it would be lots of fun, Tracy, but I'm sorry, it's just not going to happen," Elaine said.

She tried to give me a big hug but I pushed her hard.

"I was only joking," I said. "Yuck. I couldn't

stand the thought of living with you. You're stupid and boring and you're all fat and wobbly. I'd absolutely hate the idea of you being my foster mom."

"I can understand why you're angry with me, Tracy," said Elaine, trying to look cool and calm but sucking in her stomach all the same.

I told her I wasn't a bit angry, though I shouted as I said it. I told her I didn't care a bit, though I had these silly watery eyes. I didn't cry, though. I don't *ever* cry. Sometimes people think I do, but it's my hay fever.

"I expect you're going to think up all sorts of revolting curses for me now," said Elaine.

"I'm doing it right this minute," I told her.

"Okay," she said.

"You always say okay," I told her. "You know: 'Okay, that's fine with me, if that's what you want I'm not going to make a fuss; okay, Tracy, yes, I know you've got this great big ax in your hand and you're about to chop off my head because you're feeling angry with me, but okay, if that's the way you feel, I'm not going to get worried about it because I'm this supercool social worker.'"

She burst out laughing then.

"No one can stay supercool when you're around, Tracy," she said. "Look, kiddo, you write whatever you want in your life story. It's your own book, after all."

So that's that. This is my own book and I can write whatever I want. Only I'm not quite sure what

I do want, actually. Maybe Elaine *could* help after all. She's over on the other side of the living room, helping that dumb Peter with his book. He hasn't got a clue. He's filling it all in *so* slowly and *so* seriously, not writing it but printing it with that silly blotchy ballpoint pen of his, trying to do it ever so carefully but failing miserably, and now he's smudged some of it so it looks like a mess anyway.

I've just called Elaine but she says she's got to help Peter for a while. The poor little petal is getting all worried in case he puts the wrong answers, as if it's some dopey intelligence test. I've done heaps of them, intelligence tests. They're all ever so easy-peasy. I can do them quick as a wink. They always expect kids in foster care to be as thick as bricks, but I get a hundred out of a hundred nearly every time. Well, they don't tell you the answers, but I bet I get everything right.

TRACY BEAKER IS A STUPID SHOW-OFF AND THIS IS THE SILLIEST LOAD OF RUBBISH I'VE EVER READ AND IF SHE'S SO SUPER-INTELLIGENT HOW COME SHE WETS HER BED LIKE A BABY ?

Ignore the stupid scribble up above. It's all lies anyway. It's typical. You can't leave anything for two minutes in this rotten place without one of the other kids spoiling it. But I never thought anyone would stoop so low as to write in my own private life story. And I know who did it too. I know, Justine Littlewood, and you just wait. I'm going to get you.

I went over to rescue Elaine from that boring wimpy little Peter and I had a sneak peek into his book and I nearly fell over, because you'll never guess who he's put as his best friend. Me. *Me!*

"Is this some sort of joke?" I demanded. He went all red and mumbly and tried to hide what he'd put, but I'd already seen it. *My best friend is Tracy Beaker.* It was down there on the page in black and white. Well, not your actual black and white, more your smudgy blue ballpoint, but you know what I mean.

"Go away and stop pestering poor Peter," Elaine said to me.

"Yes, but he's putting absolute rubbish in his

book, Elaine, and it's stupid. I'm not Peter Ingham's best friend!"

"Well, I think it's very nice that Peter wants you to be his friend," said Elaine. She made a funny face. "There's no accounting for taste."

"Oh, ha-ha. Why did you put that, Peter?"

Peter squeaked a little about sharing birthdays and so that made us friends.

"It does *not* make us friends, dumbo," I declared.

Elaine started getting on my case then, saying I was being nasty to poor little Peetie-Weetie and if I couldn't be friendly why didn't I just shove off and get on with my own life story? Well, when people tell me to shove off I generally try to stick to them like glue, just to be annoying, so that's what I did.

And then Jenny called me into the kitchen because she made out she wanted a hand getting the lunch ready, but that was just a *ploy*. Jenny doesn't smack. She doesn't even often tell you off. She just uses ploys and tries to distract you. It sometimes works with the thicker kids but it usually has no effect whatsoever on me. However, I quite like helping in the kitchen because you can generally steal a spoonful of jam or a handful of raisins when Jenny's back is turned. So I went along to the kitchen and helped her put an entire package of fish fingers under the broiler while she got the pan for the french fries bubbling. Fish fingers don't taste so great when they're raw. I tried nibbling just to see. I don't know why they're called fish *fingers*. Fish don't have fingers, do they? These things ought to be called fish *fins*. That Auntie Peggy used to make this awful milk pudding called tapioca, which had these little slimy bubbly bits, and I told the other kids that they were fish eyes. And I told the really little ones that marmalade is made out of goldfish and they believed that too.

When Jenny started serving the fish fingers and fries, I went back into the living room to tell everyone that lunch was ready. And I remember seeing Louise and Justine hunched up in a corner, giggling over something they'd got hidden. I don't know. I *am* highly intelligent, I truly wasn't making that up, and yet it was a bit thick of me not to get what they were up to. Which was reading my own life story and then scribbling all over it.

A little twit like Peter Ingham would tell, but I'm no tattletale. I'll simply get them back. I'll think long and carefully for a suitably horrible revenge. I really hate that Justine. Before she came, Louise and I were best friends and we did everything together and, even though I was still dumped in a rotten children's home, it really wasn't so bad. Louise and I made out we were sisters and we had all these secrets and . . .

One of these secrets was about a certain small problem that I have. A nighttime problem. I've got my own room and so it was always a private prob-

25

lem that only Jenny and I knew about. Only to show
Louise we were the bestest friends ever I told her
about it. I knew it wasn't a sensible move right from
the start because she giggled, and she used to tease
me about it a bit even when we were still friends.
And then she went off with Justine and I'd sometimes worry that she might tell on me, but I always
convinced myself she'd never ever stoop that low.
Not Louise.

But she has told. She's told Justine, my worst enemy. So what am I
going to do to her? Any ideas ticking
away inside my head?

Well, I could beat her up.

Tick, tick, tick.
I could deliver a karate-chop death blow.

Tick, tick, tick.
I could get my mom to come in her car and run
her over, squashing her flat as roadkill.

Tick, tick, tick. Hey! Tick tock. Tick tock. *I* know. And I also know I'm not leaving this book around. From now on I'll carry it on my person. So, ha-ha, boo to you, Justine Littlewood. Oh, you're going to get it. Yes you are, yes you are, tee-hee.

I'm writing this at midnight. I can't put the light on because Jenny might still be prowling about and I don't want *another* ding-dong with her, thanks very much. I'm making do with a flashlight, only the battery's going, so there's just this dim little glow and I can hardly see what I'm doing. I wish I had something to eat. In all those old-fashioned school stories they always have midnight feasts. The food sounds a bit weird, sardines and condensed milk, but I could demolish a Mars bar right this minute. Imagine a Mars bar as big as this bed. Imagine licking it, gnawing away at a corner, scooping out the soft part with both fists. Imagine the wonderful chocolaty smell. I'm drooling at the thought. Yes, that's what those little marks are on the page. Drool. I don't cry. I don't *ever* cry.

I acted as if I couldn't care less when Jenny got really mad. And I don't.

"I think you really do care, Tracy," she said, in that silly sorrowful voice. "Deep down I think you're really very sorry."

"That's just where you're wrong," I insisted.

"Come off it now. You must know how you'd feel if your mother had bought you a special present and one of the other kids spoiled it."

As she said that I couldn't help remembering being in the first Home, long before the dreaded Auntie Peggy or that mean hateful unfair Julie and Ted. My mom came to see me and she'd brought this doll, a doll almost as big as me, with long golden curls and a bright blue lacy dress to match her big blue eyes. I'd never liked dolls all that much but I thought this one was wonderful. I called her Bluebell and I undressed her right down to her frilly white panties and dressed her up again and brushed her blond curls and made her blink her big blue eyes, and at night she'd lie in my bed and we'd have these cozy little chats and she'd tell me that Mom was coming back really soon, probably tomorrow, and—

Okay, that sort of thing makes me want to puke now but I was only little then and I didn't know any better. The housemother let me cart Bluebell all over the place but she tried to make me give the other kids a turn playing with her. Well, I wasn't going to let that bunch maul her, so of course I didn't let them hold her. But I came unglued when I started school. You weren't allowed to take toys to school, only on Friday afternoons. I cried and fought but they wouldn't let me. So I had to start leaving Bluebell at home. I'd tuck her up in my bed with her eyes closed, pretending she was asleep, and then when I got home from school I'd charge upstairs into our crummy little dormitory and wake her up with a big hug.

29

Only one day I woke her up and I got the shock of my life. Her eyelids snapped open but her blue eyes had vanished inside her head. Some rotten lousy pig had given them a good poke. I couldn't stand it, seeing those creepy empty sockets. She stopped being my friend. She just scared me.

The housemother took Bluebell off to this doll hospital and they gave her some new eyes. They were blue too, but not the same bright blue, and they didn't blink properly either. They either got stuck altogether or they flashed up and down all the time, making her look silly and fluttery. But I didn't really care then. She was spoiled. She wasn't the same Bluebell. She didn't talk to me anymore.

I never found out which kid had done it. The housemother said it was A Mystery. Just One of Those Things.

Jenny didn't call it a mystery when Justine went sobbing to her because her silly old Mickey Mouse alarm clock had got broken. Clocks break all the time. It's not as if it's a really glitzy, expensive clock. If I'd been Jenny I'd have told Justine to stop making such a silly fuss. I'd have stopped up my ears when that sneaky little twerp started going on about me. "I bet I know who did it too, Jenny. *That Tracy Beaker.*"

Yes, she told on me. And Jenny listened, because she came looking for me. She had to look quite a long time. I kind of suspected what was coming, so I ran away. I didn't try to hide in the house or the garden like one of the little kids. I'm not that dumb. They can flush you out in five minutes no matter where you are. No, I skipped out the back door and down the road and wandered around the town.

It was great. Yes, I had the most amazing time. First I went to McDonald's and had a Big Mac and french fries with a strawberry milk shake and then I went to the movies and saw this really funny film and I laughed so much I fell out of my seat and then I went off with this whole crowd of friends to an amusement arcade and I kept winning the jackpot on the fruit machines and then we all went off to

this party and I drank a whole bottle of wine and it was great, it just tasted like lemonade, and this girl there, we made friends and she asked me if I'd like to stay the night, sharing her twin beds in this fantastic pink-and-white room, in fact she said I could stay there permanently if I really wanted and so I said . . .

I said: "No thanks, I'd sooner go back to my crummy children's home."

Of course I didn't say that. Well, she didn't say it either. I sort of made her up. And her party. I didn't go down to the amusement arcade. Or to the movies. Or McDonald's. I *would* have gone, but I couldn't, on account of the fact that I ran off with no cash whatsoever.

I said I tell fibs sometimes. It makes things more interesting. I mean, what's the point of writing what I really did? Which was loaf about the town feeling more and more fed up. The only thing I could think of doing was to sit in the bus shelter. It got a bit boring. I pretended I was waiting for a bus and I tried to think of all the places I'd like to go to. But that began to depress me because I started thinking about Watford, where my mom said she lived. And last year I got enough money together (which created a few problems afterward, since I sort of borrowed it without asking) and figured out the journey and took all these trains and buses and all the rest of it, so that I could pay my mom a visit and give her a lovely surprise. Only it was me that got the surprise because she wasn't there. The people who lived in that house said she'd moved about six months ago and they didn't have a clue where she'd gone.

So it's going to take a bit of organized searching to find her again. I could catch a different bus every day for the rest of my life and maybe not find her. It's hard when you haven't got a clue where to look.

I was still scrunched up in the bus shelter when a familiar white minivan hove into view. It was Mike, come looking for me. Mike looks after us with Jenny. He's such a bore. He doesn't often get angry but he whines on about Rules and Responsibility and a whole lot of other rubbish.

So by the time I'd got back to the Home I was sick to death of the subject, but then Jenny came into my bedroom and *she* started. And she assumed it was me that broke Justine's clock though she had no proof whatsoever. I told her so, and said she just liked picking on me, and it wasn't fair. She said I'd feel better if I owned up to breaking Justine's clock and then went to apologize to her. I said she had to be joking. I wasn't the slightest bit sorry and anyway I didn't didn't *didn't* break Justine's rotten clock.

That isn't necessarily a fib. I don't absolutely one hundred percent *know* that I broke it. All right, I did go into her bedroom when she was in the bathroom, and I did pick up the clock to look at it. Well, she's always going on about it because she's got this boring thing about her dad. She makes out he's so flipping special, when he hardly ever comes to see her. The only thing he's ever given her is that stupid tinny old alarm clock. I wanted to look at it to see if it was really so special. Well, it wasn't. I bet he just got it from some cheap discount store. And it certainly wasn't made very carefully because when I twiddled the knobs to make the little Mickey on the end of the hands go whizzing around and around he couldn't keep it up for very long. There was this sudden whir and clunk and then the hand fell off altogether and Mickey fell too, with his little paws in the air, dead.

But he might have been about to take his last gasp anyway. That hand might well have fallen off the next time Justine touched the stupid clock to wind it up.

I'm not going to say I'm sorry no matter what.

I wish I could get to sleep.

I'll try counting sheep . . .

I *still* can't get to sleep and it's the middle of the night now and it's rotten and I keep thinking about my mom. I wish she'd come and get me. I wish anyone would come and get me. Why can't I ever get a good foster family? That Auntie Peggy and Uncle Sid were lousy. But then I could figure them out and tell they were lousy right from the start. Anyone who smacks hard and serves up fish eyes in your pudding is certainly not an ideal auntie. But last time, when I got taken in by Julie and Ted, I really thought it was all going to work out happily ever

after, and that it was my turn to be the golden
princess instead of a Rumpelstiltskin.

They were great at first, Julie and Ted. That's what
I called them right from the start. They didn't want
to be a prissy auntie and uncle. And Julie said she
didn't want me to call her Mom because I already
had a mom. I thought such a lot of Julie when she
said that. She wasn't exactly my idea of a glamorous
foster mom—she had this long wispy brown hair
and she wore sludge-colored smocks and sandals—
and Ted looked like a bit of a wimp too with his
glasses and his beard and weirdo comfy walking
shoes. Not so much Hush Puppy as Shut-your-face

Hound-Dog—but I thought they were the sort of couple you could really trust. Ha!

I went to live with them and I thought we were getting on really great, though they were a bit boringly strict about stuff like sweets and bedtimes and horror videos, but then Julie started to wear bigger smocks than ever and lolled about on the sofa and Ted got all misty-eyed behind his glasses and I started to realize that something was up. And so I asked them what it was and they hedged and made faces at each other and then they looked shifty and told me that everything was fine and I knew they were lying. Things weren't fine at all.

They didn't even have the guts to tell me themselves. They left it to Elaine. She'd only just started to be my social worker then (I've had heaps because they kept moving around and leaving me behind and I got passed on like a parcel). I wasn't that keen on Elaine in those days. In fact I was really annoyed with her, because I'd had this man social worker Terry before her and he used to call me Smartie and he used to give me the odd package of Smarties too, and I felt Elaine was a very poor substitute.

I wish I hadn't thought of those Smarties. I wish I had some now, I'm simply starving.

I'm sure Elaine marked me down as Sulky and Noncooperative in her little notebook. The day she told me the Julie and Ted Bombshell I'm sure she scribbled TRACY TOTALLY STUNNED. Because Julie was having her own baby, after years of thinking she couldn't have any kids.

I didn't get it at first.

"So what's the problem, Elaine?" I said. "We'll be a proper family then, four of us instead of three."

Elaine was having difficulty finding the right words. She kept opening her mouth and closing it again, not saying a thing.

"You look just like a fish when you do that, did you know?" I said rudely, because my heart was starting to hammer hard against my chest and I knew that when Elaine eventually got the words out I wouldn't like the sound of them.

"The thing is, Tracy . . . Well, Julie and Ted have loved fostering you, and they've grown very fond of you, but . . . you see, now that they're having their own baby they feel that they're not really going to be able to cope."

"Oh, I get it," I said, in this jokey silly voice. "So they're going to give the boring old baby away because they can't cope with it. And keep me. Because they had me first, didn't they?"

"Tracy—"

"They're not really going to dump me, are they?"

"They still very much want to keep in touch with you and—"

"So why can't I go on living with them? Look, I'll help all I can. Julie doesn't need to worry. I'll be just like a second mom to this baby. I know all what to do. I can give it its bottle and change its soggy old diaper and thump it on its back to burp it. I'm totally experienced where babies are concerned."

"Yes, I know, Tracy. But that's the trouble. You see, when Julie and Ted first chose you, we did tell them a bit about your background, and the trouble you had in your first foster home. You know, when you shut the baby up in the cupboard—"

"That was Steve. And he wasn't a baby. He was a foul little toddler, and he kept messing up our bedroom so I put him in the closet just for a bit so I could get everything straightened out."

"And there was the ghost game that got totally out of hand—"

"Oh, that! All those little kids *loved* that game. I was ever so good at finding the right hiding places and then I'd start an eerie sort of moan and then I'd jump out at them, wearing this old white sheet."

"And everyone got scared silly."

"No they didn't. They just squealed because they were excited. *I* was the one who should have been scared, because they were all the ghost-busters, you see, and I was the poor little ghost and—"

"Okay, okay, but the point is, Tracy, it makes it plain in your records that you don't always get on well with little children."

"That's a big fat lie! What about Camilla? I looked after her at that children's home and she loved me, she really did."

"Yes, I'm sure that's true, Tracy, but—Well, the thing is, Julie and Ted still feel they don't want to take any chances. They're worried that you might feel a bit uncomfortable with a baby in the house."

"So they're pushing me out?"

"But like I said, they still want to keep in touch with you and maybe take you out for dinner sometimes."

"No way," I said. "I don't want to see them ever again."

"Oh, Tracy, that's silly. That's just cutting off your own nose to spite your face," said Elaine.

That's such a stupid expression. How on earth would you go about it?

It sure would hurt.

It hurt a lot leaving Julie and Ted's. They wanted me to stay for a few months but I couldn't get out of there quick enough. So here I am in this dump. They've tried to see me twice but I wasn't having any of it. I don't want any visitors, thanks very much. Apart from my mom. I wonder where she is. And why didn't she leave a forwarding address at that last place? And how will she ever get to find me here? Yeah, that's the problem. I bet she's been trying and trying to get hold of me, but she doesn't know where to look. Last time I saw her I was at Auntie Peggy's. I bet Mom's been around to Auntie Peggy's and I bet that silly old smacking machine wouldn't tell her where I'd gone. So I bet my mom got really mad at her. And if she found out just how many times that Auntie Peggy smacked me then WOW! KER-POW! SPLAT! BANG! I bet my mom would really let her have it.

I want my mom so much.

I know why I can't sleep. It's because I'm so starving hungry, that's why. Crying always makes me hungry. Not that I've been crying now. I don't *ever* cry.

I think maybe I'll try slipping down to the kitchen. Jenny's bound to be fast asleep by now. Yeah, that's what I'll do.

I'm back. I've had my very own midnight feast. And it was absolutely delicious too. Well, it wasn't bad. I couldn't find any chocolate, of course, and that was what I really wanted. But I found an opened package of cornflakes and got into them, and then I tried raiding the fridge. There weren't too many goodies. I didn't pig out on tomorrow's raw hamburger or yesterday's cold custard, but I poked my finger in the butter and then dabbled it in the sugar bowl and that tasted fine. I did quite a lot of poking and dabbling, actually. I knew Jenny might notice so I got my little fingernail and drew these weeny lines like teethmarks and then did some paw prints all over the butter, so she'd think it was a mouse. Mice do eat butter, don't they? They like cheese, which is the same sort of thing. Of course this is going to have to be a mountaineering mouse, armed with ice pick and climbing boots, able to trek

up the grim north face of the refrigerator. And then it's got to develop Mighty Mouse muscles to pry open the door of the fridge to get at the feast inside.

Maybe Jenny will still be a teensy bit suspicious.

But I can't help that. At least she didn't catch me while I was noshing away at my midnight feast.

Someone else did, though. Not in the kitchen. Afterward, when I was sneaking up the stairs again. They're very dark, these stairs, and they take a bit of careful negotiating. One of the little kids is quite likely to leave a teddy bear or a rattle or a wooden block halfway up and you can have an awfully bad fall and wake the entire household. So I was feeling my way very very cautiously when I heard this weird little moaning sound coming from up on the landing. I looked up quickly, and I could just make out this pale little figure, all white and trailing, and it was so exactly like a ghost that I opened my mouth to scream.

But Tracy Beaker has a lot of guts. I'm not scared of anybody. Not even ghosts. So I clapped my hand over my mouth to stop the scream and pattered right on up the stairs to confront this puny little piece of ectoplasm. Only it wasn't a ghost after all. It was just sniveling, driveling Peter Ingham, clutching some sheets.

"Whatever are you up to, creep?" I whispered.

"Nothing," Peter whispered back.

"Oh, sure. You just thought you'd take your sheets for a walk in the middle of the night," I said.

Peter flinched away from me.

"You've wet them, haven't you?" I said.

"No," Peter mumbled. He's a useless liar.

"Of course you've wet them. And you've been try-

43

ing to wash them out in the bathroom, I know. So that people won't guess."

"Oh, don't tell, Tracy, please," Peter begged.

"What do you take me for? I'm no tattletale," I said. "And look, you don't have to fuss. Just get Jenny by herself in the morning and whisper to her. She'll take care of it for you. She doesn't get angry."

"Really?"

"Truly. And what you do now, you get yourself some dry sheets from the linen closet, right? And some pajamas. Goodness, you don't know anything, do you? How long have you been in foster care?"

"Three months, one week, two days," said Peter.

"Is that all? I've been in and out of children's homes nearly all my life," I said, getting the sheets for him. "So then why are you here now? Your mom and dad get fed up with you? Can't say I blame them."

"They died when I was little. So I lived with my granny. But then she got old and then—then she died too," Peter mumbled. "And I didn't have any-one else so I had to come here. And I don't like it."

"Well, of course you don't like it. But this is a lot better than most children's homes. You ought to have tried some of the places I've been in. They lock you up and they beat you and they practically starve you to death and then when they do give you meals it's absolutely disgusting, they pretend it's meat but it's really chopped-up worms and dried dog turds and—"

"Shut up, Tracy," Peter said, holding his stomach.

44

"Who are you telling to shut up?" I said, but not really fiercely. "Go on, you'd better go back to your room. And put your dry pajamas on. You're shivering."

"Okay, Tracy. Thanks." He paused, fidgeting and fumbling with his sheets. "I wish you would be my friend, Tracy."

"I don't really bother making friends," I said. "There's not much point, because my mom's probably coming to get me soon and then I'll be living with her so I won't need any friends here."

"Oh," said Peter, and he sounded really disappointed.

"Still, I suppose you can be my friend just for now," I said.

I don't know why I said it. Who wants to be saddled with a silly little creep like that? I'm too kindhearted, that's my trouble.

There wasn't much point in getting to sleep, because when I did eventually nod off I just had these stupid nightmares. It's as if there's a video inside my head and it switches itself on the minute my eyes close. I keep hoping it's going to be showing this great comedy that'll have me in stitches but then the creepy music starts and I know I'm in for it. Last night was the Great Horror Movie of all time. I was stuck in the dark somewhere and there was something really scary coming up quick behind me so I had to run like mad. Then I got to this big round pool and there were these stepping-stones with people perching on them and I jumped

45

onto the first one and there was no room at all because that fat Auntie Peggy was spread all over it. I tried to cling to her but she gave me a big smack and sent me flying. So then I jumped onto the next stepping-stone and Julie and Ted were there and I tried to grab hold of them but they just turned their backs on me and didn't even try to catch me when I fell and so I had to try to reach the next stepping-stone but I was in the water doing my doggy paddle and it was getting harder and harder, and every time I swam to a stepping-stone all these people prodded at me with sticks and pushed me away and I kept going under the water and . . .

. . . and then I woke up and I know that whenever I dream about water it spells Trouble with a capital T. I had to make my own dash to the linen closet and the laundry basket. I was unfortunate enough to bump into Justine too. She didn't look as if she'd slept much either. Her eyes seemed a bit on the red side. I couldn't help feeling a bit mean then, in spite of everything. So I gave her this big smile and I said, "I'm sorry about what happened to your alarm clock, Justine."

I didn't exactly tell her that *I* did it. Because I still don't know that it really was me. And anyway, I'd be a fool to admit it, wouldn't I? But I told her that I was still sorry, just like Jenny had suggested.

Only there's no point trying to be nice to pigs like Justine Littlewood. She didn't smile back and graciously accept my apologies.

"You'll be even sorrier when I've finished with you, Tracy Beaker," she hissed. "And what have you been doing, eh? Wet the bed again? Baby!" She hissed a lot more too. Stupid insulting things. I'm not going to waste my time writing them all down. Words can't hurt me anyway. Only I can't help being just a bit worried about that threat. What's she going to do to get back at me for the clock? If only we had those dumb locks on our bedroom doors. Still, at least we've got separate bedrooms in this Home, even though they're weeny like closets.

It's new policy. Children in foster care need their own space. And I want to stay in my own space, doing all this writing, but Jenny has just put her head around my door and told me to buzz out into the garden with the others. And I said No Fear. Being in a children's home is lousy at the best of times, but I just can't take it during school vacations when you're all cooped up together and the big ones bully you and the little ones pester you and the ones your own age gang up on you and have secrets together and call you names.

"How's about trying to make up with Justine?" Jenny suggested, coming to sit on my bed.

So I snorted and told her she was wasting her time, and more to the point, she was wasting *my* time, because I wanted to get on with my writing.

"You've done ever such a lot, Tracy," said Jenny, looking at all these pages. "We'll be running out of paper soon."

"Then I'll use the backs of birthday cards. Or a roll of toilet paper. Anything. I'm inspired, see. I can't stop."

"Yes, you've really taken to this writing. Going to be a writer when you grow up, eh?"

"Maybe." I hadn't thought about it before. I was always sure I was going to be on TV with my own talk show. *The Tracy Beaker Experience*. I'd walk out onto this stage in a sparkly dress and all the studio audience would clap and cheer and all these really famous celebrities would fight tooth and nail to get on my show to speak to me. But I reckon I could write books too.

"Tell you what, Tracy. We've got a real writer coming by sometime this afternoon. You could ask her for a few tips."

"What's she coming for?"

"Oh, she's doing this article for a magazine about children in foster care."

"Oh, that boring old stuff," I said, pretending to yawn, but inside I started fizzing away.

I wouldn't mind my story being written up in some magazine. A book would be better, of course, but maybe that could come later. I'd have to be careful what she said about me, though. Elaine the Pain made a real mess of my newspaper ad. I was Child of the Week in the local paper. If she'd only let me write it I'd have been bowled over by

people rushing to adopt dear little Tracy Beaker. I
know just how to present myself in the right sort
of way.

TRACY BEAKER

HAVE YOU A PLACE IN YOUR
HEARTS FOR DEAR LITTLE TRACY?
BRILLIANT AND BEAUTIFUL, THIS
LITTLE GIRL NEEDS A LOVING
HOME. VERY RICH PARENTS PREFERRED,
AS LITTLE TRACY NEEDS LOTS OF
TOYS, PRESENTS AND PETS TO
MAKE UP FOR HER TRAGIC PAST.

Elaine is useless. Doesn't have a clue. She didn't
even let me get specially dressed up for the photo-
graph.

"We want you looking natural, Tracy," she said.

Well, I turned out looking too flipping natural.
Hair all over the place and a scowl on my face
because that stupid photographer kept treating me
like a baby, telling me to Watch the Birdie. And the
things Elaine wrote about me!

I ask you!

"How could you *do* this to me, Elaine?" I shrieked
when I saw it. "Is that the best thing you can say

TRACY

Tracy is a lively, healthy, chatty ten-year-old who has been in foster care for a number of years. Consequently she has a few behavior problems and needs firm, loving handling in a long-term foster home.

about me? That I'm *healthy*? And anyway, I'm not. What about my hay fever?"

"I also say you're lively. And chatty."

"Yeah. Well, we all know what that means. Rude. Difficult. Bossy."

"You said it, Tracy," Elaine murmured.

"And all this stuff about behavior problems! What do I do, eh? I don't go around beating people up. Well, not many. And I don't smash the furniture. Hardly ever."

"Tracy, it's very understandable that you have a few problems—"

"I *don't*! And then how could you ask for someone to handle me *firmly*?"

"And lovingly," said Elaine. "I put 'loving' too."

"Oh yes, they'll tell me how much they love me as

they lay into me with a cane. Honestly, Elaine, you've gone around the bend. You're just going to attract a bunch of creepy child-beaters with this crummy ad."

But it didn't even attract them. No one replied at all.

Elaine kept telling me not to worry, as if it was somehow my fault. I know if she'd only get her act together and do a really flashy ad there'd be heaps of offers. I bet.

But maybe I'm wasting my time nagging Elaine. This woman who's coming this afternoon might be just the chance I've been waiting for. If she's a real writer, then she'll know how to jazz it all up so that I sound really fantastic. Only I've got to present myself to her in a special way so that she'll pick me out from all the others and just do a feature on me. So what am I going to do, eh?

Aha!

Not aha. More like boo-hoo. Only I don't ever cry, of course.

I don't want to write down what happened. I don't think I want to be a writer anymore.

I tried, I really did. I went flying up to my bedroom straight after lunch and I did my best to make myself look pretty. I know my hair is untidy so I tried scragging it back into these little stick-out braids. Camilla had little braids and everyone cooed over them and said how cute she looked. I thought my face looked a bit plain when

I'd done the braids so I wetted some of the side hairs with spit and tried to make them go into curls.

I still looked a bit boring so I decided to liven my face up a bit. I sneaked into Adele's room. She's sixteen and she's got a Saturday job. Her drawer is absolutely chockful of makeup. I borrowed a bit of blusher to give myself some color in my cheeks. And then I thought I'd try out a pink glossy lipstick too. And mascara to make my eyelashes look long. I tried a bit on my eyebrows too, to make them stand out. And I put a lot of powder on to be like the icing on a cake. I thought I looked okay when I'd finished. Well, at least I looked different.

I changed my clothes too. I didn't want this writer to see me in a scrubby old T-shirt and skirt. No way. It had to be nice dress time. Only I don't really have a nice dress of my own. I did try on a few of Adele's things but somehow they didn't really suit me.

So then I started thinking about all the other girls. Louise had this really fantastic dress that she got a couple of years ago from some auntie. A really nice party dress with smocking and a flouncy skirt and its own sewn-in frilly white petticoat. It was a bit small for her now, of course, but she could just about squeeze into it for special days. And Louise and I are about the same size.

I knew Louise would get really upset if she saw me parading around in her best party dress, but I decided it might be worth it if I made a great impression on the writer woman first. So I scurried along the corridor toward her room, but I didn't have any luck. Louise was in her room. With Justine. I heard their voices.

They were discussing me, actually. And diapers. They were snorting with laughter and normally I'd have marched right in and punched their silly smirky faces but I knew if I got into a fight Jenny would send me to my room and make me stay there and I'd miss out on meeting the woman writer.

So with *extreme* self-control I walked away, still musing on what I was going to wear. I know it's summer, but I'd started to feel a bit shaky and shivery so I put on this mohair sweater that Julie knitted me for Christmas. When Julie and Ted dumped me I vowed not to have anything to do with them and I even thought about cutting up the mohair sweater into little woolly hankies but I couldn't quite do it. It's a pretty fantastic sweater, actually, with the name Tracy in bright blue letters. That way it's obvious it's mine, specially made for me. Of course it's a bit tickly and prickly, but my mom once said you have to suffer if you want to look beautiful.

She's always looked beautiful. I really wish I took after her. I wasn't too bad as a baby. I was still quite cute as a toddler. But then I changed in a big way.

Still, I was trying my hardest to look okay. I only had my old skirt to wear with my mohair sweater, and there were dark blue stains all down one side where a ballpoint pen exploded in my pocket, but I couldn't help that. The woman writer might just think it was a tie-dye effect. And at least the blue matched the lettering on my sweater.

I kept on primping and preening in my room. I heard all the other kids go clattering downstairs. I heard Louise and Justine go giggle-snigger-titter along the corridor. My face started burning so that I didn't need my blusher. Then I heard Adele rampaging around because some rotten so-and-so had been in her room and rifled through all her makeup and messed it all up. I decided to hang around in my room a bit longer.

I heard the front doorbell. I heard Jenny talking to someone down in the hall. I heard them go into the living room. I knew it was time to make my Entrance.

So I went running down the stairs and barged into the living room with this great big smile on my face. It's no use looking sad or sulky if you want people to like you. Mom always tells me to give her a big smile. Even when she's saying goodbye to me. You can't look gloomy or it just upsets people and they don't want any more to do with you.

You've got to have this great big s-s-s-m-m-m-i-i-i-l-l-l-e-e-e.

Everyone looked up at me when I went into the living room. And they all smiled too. Just for a moment I was crazy enough to think they were all smiling back at me. But then I saw they were the wrong sort of smiles. They were smirks. And Justine and Louise nudged each other and giggled and spluttered and whooped. And Adele glared at me. Peter Ingham was the only one with a proper smile. He came over to me. He was blinking a bit rapidly.

"You look . . . nice, Tracy," he said.

But I knew he was lying. It was no use kidding myself. It was obvious I looked like a total idiot. Jenny's pretty laid back about appearances but even she looked shocked at the sight of me. And it looked like all that effort was for nothing, because she didn't seem to have the woman writer person with her after all.

I've seen women writers on talk shows on TV. They're quite glamorous, like movie stars, with glittery dresses and high heels and lots of jewelry. They look a bit like my mom, only nowhere near as pretty, of course.

The woman with Jenny looked like some boring

57

social worker or teacher. Scruffy brown hair. No makeup. Scrubby T-shirt and rumpled jeans. A bit like me on an off day, grown up.

I decided to slink back to my bedroom. It seemed sensible to steer clear of Adele anyway. But Jenny caught hold of me by the back of my sweater.

"Hang around, Tracy. I thought you wanted to meet Cam Lawson."

"Who?" I said.

"You know. The writer. I told you," Jenny said through her teeth. Then she lowered her voice even more. "Why are you wearing your winter sweater when it's boiling hot today? And what on earth have you done to your face?"

"She thinks she looks pretty," said Justine, and she clutched Louise and they both shrieked.

"Pipe down, you two," said Jenny. "Tracy. Tracy!" She hung on to me firmly, stopping me from barging over to that stupid pair of titterers so that I could bang their heads together. "Leave them, Tracy. Come and meet Cam."

I wanted to meet this Cam (what sort of a silly name is that?) even though she didn't look a bit like a *proper* writer, but I sort of hung back. I'm usually the last person to feel shy, but somehow I suddenly didn't know what to say or what to do. So I growled something at Jenny and twisted away from her and stood in a corner by myself, just watching.

Peter came trotting after me. Justine and Louise were still having hysterics at my appearance. You

58

could tell they'd actually got over the giggles by this time, but Justine kept going into further false whoops and Louise was almost as bad.

"Don't take any notice of them," Peter whispered.

"I don't," I said angrily.

"I like your sweater," said Peter. "And your makeup. And the new hairstyle."

"Then you're crazy. It's a mess. I'm a mess. I look like a mess *on purpose*," I said fiercely. "So you needn't feel sorry for me, Peter Ingham. You just get out of here and leave me alone, right?"

Peter fidgeted from one foot to the other, looking worried.

"Get out of here, you stupid little creep," I said.

So of course he did leave then. I wondered why I'd said it. Okay, he *is* a creep, but he's not really that bad. I'd said he could be my friend. And it was a lot better when he was with me than standing all by myself, watching everyone over on the other side of the room clustered around this Cam person calling herself a writer.

She's a weird sort of woman, if you ask me. She was chatting away and yet you could tell she was really nervous inside. She kept fidgeting with her pen and notebook and I was amazed to see she bites her nails! She's a great big grown-up woman and yet she does a dopey kid's thing like that. Well, she's not great big, she's little and skinny, but even so!

My mom has the most beautiful fingernails, very long and pointy and shiny. She polishes them every day. I just love that smell of nail polish, that sharp

smell that makes your nostrils twitch. Jenny caught me happily sniffing nail polish one day, and do you know what she thought? That I was inhaling it, like sniffing glue. Did you ever? I let her think it too. *I* wasn't going to tell her I just liked the smell because it reminds me of Mom.

I'll tell you another weird thing about Cam What-sit. She sat on one of our rickety old chairs, her legs all draped around the rungs, and she talked *to* the children. Most adults that come here talk *at* children.

They tell you what to do.

They go on and on about themselves.

They talk about you.

They ask endless stupid questions.

They make personal comments.

Even the social workers do it. Or they strike this special nothing-you-can-say-would-shock-

me-sweetie pose and they make stupid state-
ments.

"I guess you're feeling really angry and upset
today, Tracy," they twitter, when I've wrecked my
bedroom or got into a fight or shouted and sworn
at someone, so that it's *obvious* I'm angry and
upset.

They do this to show me that they understand.
Only they don't understand peanuts. *They're* not the
ones in foster care. I am.

I thought Cam Thing would ask questions and
take down case histories in her notebook, all brisk
and organized. But from what I could make out
over in the corner she had a very different way of
doing things.

She smiled a bit and fidgeted a lot and sort of
checked everybody out, and they all had a good
stare at her. Two of the little kids tried to climb up
onto her lap because they do that to anyone who sits
down. It's not because they *like* the person, it's just
they like being cuddled. They'd cry to cuddle with a
cross-eyed gorilla, I'm telling you.

Most strangers to children's homes get all flat-
tered and make a great fuss of the little kids and
come on like Mary Poppins. This Cam seemed a bit
surprised, even a bit put out. I don't blame her. Little Wayne in particular has got the runniest nose of
all time and he likes to bury his head affectionately
in your chest, wiping it all down your front.

Cam held him at arm's length, and when he tried
his burrowing trick she distracted him by giving

61

him her pen. He liked flicking the catch up and down.

She let little Becky have a ride on her foot at the same time so she didn't feel left out and bawl. Becky kept trying to climb up her leg, pulling her jeans up. Some of Cam's leg got exposed. It was a pretty lousy sort of leg if you ask me. A bit hairy, for a start. My mom always shaves her legs, and she wears sheer pantyhose to show them off. This Cam had socks like a schoolgirl. Only they were quite funny, brightly patterned socks. I thought the red-and-yellow bits were just squares at first, but then I got a bit closer and saw they were books. I wouldn't mind having a pair of socks like that myself, if I'm going to write all these books.

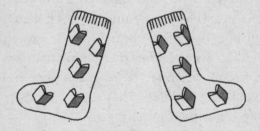

She's written books, this Cam. The other kids asked her and she told them. She said she wrote some stories but they didn't sell much so she also wrote some romantic stuff. She doesn't look the romantic type to me.

Adele got interested then because she loves all those soppy love books and Cam told her some titles and the boys all tittered and went yuck yuck and Jenny got a bit annoyed but Cam said she didn't mind, they were mostly yucky but she couldn't help it if that's what people liked to read.

Then they all started talking about reading. Maxy said he liked this book *Where the Wild Things Are* because the boy in that is called Max, and Cam said she knew that book and she made a Wild Thing face and then everyone else did too.

Except me. I mean, I didn't want to join in a dopey game like that. My face did twitch a bit but then I remembered all the makeup and I knew I'd look really stupid.

Besides, I'd got her figured out. I could see what she was up to. She was finding out all sorts of things about all the kids without asking any nosy questions. Maxy went on about his dad being a Wild Thing. Adele went on about love, only of course real life wasn't like that, and love didn't ever last and people split up and sometimes didn't even go on loving their children.

Even little creepy Peter piped up about these books by Catherine Cookson that his granny used to like, and he told Cam how he used to read them to her because her eyes had gone all blurry. And then *his* eyes went a bit blurry too, remembering his granny, and Cam's hand reached out sort of awkwardly. She didn't quite manage to hold his hand, she just sort of tapped his bony wrist sympathetically.

"My granny's dead too. And my mom. They're both together in heaven now. Angels, like," said Louise, lisping a bit.

She always does that. Puts on this sweet little baby act when there are grown-ups about. Like she was a little angel herself. Ha. Our little Louise can be even worse than me when she wants. She's had three foster placements, no, was it four? Anyway, none of them worked out. But Louise always swore she didn't care. We used to have this pact that we'd do our best not to get fostered at all and we'd stay together at the Home till we got to be eighteen and then we'd get them to house us together. In our own modern apartment. We'd got it all planned out. Louise even started thinking about our furniture, the ornaments, the posters on the walls.

And then Justine came and everything was spoiled. Oh, how I hate that Justine Littlewood! I'm glad I broke her silly Mickey Mouse alarm clock. I'd like to break her into little bits and all.

Anyway, Louise lisped on about angels and I'll give that Cam her due, she didn't go all simpering and sentimental and pat Louise on her curly head and talk about the little darling. She stayed calm and matter-of-fact, and started talking about angels and wondering what they would look like.

"That's simple, Miss. They've got these big wings and long white nighties and those gold plate things stuck on the back of their heads," said Justine.

"Draw one for me," said Cam, offering her pen and notebook.

"Okay," said Justine, though she can't draw to save her life. Then she had a close look at the pen in her hand. "Here, it's a Mickey Mouse pen. Look, Louise, see the little Mickey. Oh, Miss, where did you get this pen? It's great! I love Mickey, I do. I've got this Mickey Mouse alarm clock, my dad gave it to me, only some *pig* broke it deliberately." Justine looked over her shoulder and glared at me.

I glared back, pretending I couldn't care less. And I *couldn't*. My face started burning, but that was just because of my mohair sweater.

Justine drew her stupid angel and Cam nodded at it.

"Yes, that's the way people usually draw angels." She looked at Louise. "So is this the way you imagine your mom and your granny?"

"Well, sort of," said Louise.

"Is that the sort of nightie that your granny would wear? And what about the halo, the gold plate part. Would that fit neatly on top of her hairstyle?"

Louise giggled uncertainly, not sure what she was getting at.

"You draw me what you think your mom and granny look like as angels," said Cam.

Louise started, but she can't draw much either, and she kept scribbling over what she'd done.

65

"This is silly," she said, giving up.

I knew what Cam was getting at. I'd have done a really great drawing of Louise's mom and granny in natty angel outfits. Like this.

"I'll draw you an angel, Miss," said Maxy, grabbing at the pen. "I'll draw me as an angel and I'll have big wings so I can fly like an airplane, y-e-e-e-o-o-o-w, y-e-e-e-o-o-o-w." He went on making his dopey airplane noises all the time he was drawing.

Then the others had a turn, even the big ones. I got a bit nearer and craned my neck to see what they'd all drawn. I didn't think any of them was very inspired.

I knew exactly what I'd draw if she asked me. It wouldn't be a silly old angel.

Then Cam looked up. She caught my eye. She did ask me.

"Have a turn?" she said, totally casual.

I gave this little shrug as if I couldn't care less. Then I sauntered forward, very slowly. I held out my hand for the pen.

"This is Tracy," said Jenny, poking her big nose in. "She's the one who wants to be a writer."

I felt my face start burning again.

"What, her?" said Justine. "You've got to be joking."

"Now Justine," said Jenny. "Tracy's written pages and pages in her Life Book."

"Yeah, but it's all rubbish," said Justine, and her hand shot out and she made a grab underneath my sweater, where I was keeping this book for safety. I lashed out at her but I wasn't quick enough. She snatched the book from me before I could stop her.

"Give that back!" I shrieked.

"It's rubbish, I tell you—listen," said Justine, and she opened my book and started reading in a silly high-pitched baby voice: "'Once upon a time there was a little girl called Tracy Beaker and that sounds stupid and no wonder because I *am* stupid and I wet the bed and—Ooooowwww!'"

Things got a bit hazy after that. But I got my book back. And Justine's nose became a wonderful scarlet fountain. I was glad glad glad. I wanted her whole body to spout blood but Jenny had hold of me by this time and she was shouting for Mike and I got hauled off to the Quiet Room. Only I wasn't quiet in there. I yelled my head off. I went on yelling when Jenny came to try and calm me down. And then Jenny went away and someone else came into the room. I wasn't sure who it was at first because when I yell my eyes screw up and I can't see properly. Then I made out the jeans and the T-shirt and the shock of hair and I knew it was Cam Whosit and that made me burn all over until I felt like a junior Joan of Arc.

There was me, throwing a hairy fit, and there was her, standing there watching me. I don't care about people like Jenny or Elaine seeing me. They're used to it. Nearly all children in foster care have a screaming session once in a while. I have them more than once, actually. And I usually just let it rip, but now I felt like a total raving loony in front of her.

But I didn't stop yelling, all the same. There was no point. She'd already seen me at it. And heard me too. She didn't try to stop me. She wasn't saying a word. She was standing there. And she had this awful expression on her face. I couldn't stand it. She looked sorry for me.

I didn't like that. So I told her to go away. That's putting it politely. I yelled some very rude words at her. And she just sort of shrugged and nodded and went away.

I was left screaming and swearing away, all by myself.

But I'm okay now. I'm not in the Quiet Room anymore. I stayed in there ever such a long time and I even had my dinner in there on a tray but now I'm in my bedroom and I've been writing and writing and writing away and it looks like I can't *help* being a writer. I've written so much I've got a big lump on the longest finger of my right hand. You look.

I used to play this crazy game with my fingers. I'd make them into a family. There were Mommy Finger and Daddy Finger, big brother Freddy Finger, pretty little Pinkie Finger, and Baby Thumbkin. I'd give myself a little puppet show with them, making them jump about, and I'd take them for walks up and down the big hill of my leg and I'd tuck them in for the night in my hankie.

Baby Camilla used to like that game ever so much. I'd give the Finger family different squeaky voices and I'd make them talk to her and take turns tapping her tiny little nose and she'd always chuckle so much her whole body jumped up and down. I really miss Camilla.

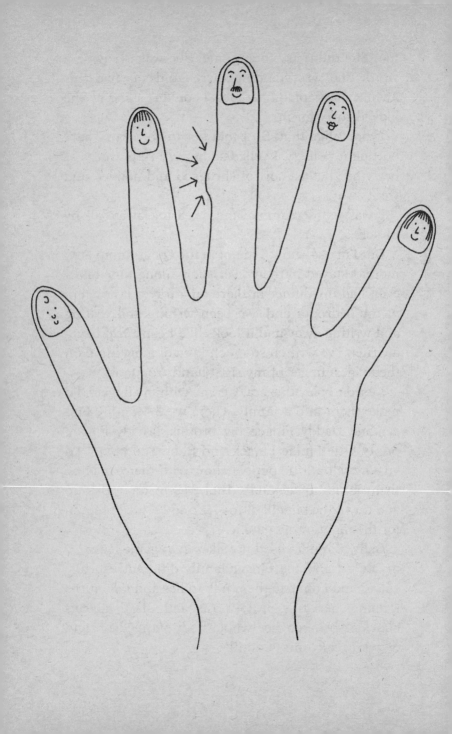

Hey. Sudden thought. Cam. Is Cam short for *Camilla*?

I was delighted at breakfast to see that Justine has a swollen nose and a Band-Aid.

The swollen nose matches her swollen head. Justine Littlewood thinks she's really *it*. And she isn't. I truly don't get what Louise sees in her. If *I* were Louise I'd much sooner be Tracy Beaker's best friend.

What really gets me is that I was the one who palled up with Justine first. She turned up at the Home one evening, all down and droopy because her mom had gone off with some guy and left Justine and her two little brothers and her dad to get on with it. Only her dad couldn't get on with it, and the kids got taken into foster care. The brothers got into a short-term foster home because they were still nearly at the baby stage and not too much bother. But Justine didn't get taken in too, because they thought she'd be difficult.

I generally like kids who are difficult. And I thought I liked the look of Justine. And the sound of her. Because after the first droopy evening she suddenly found her tongue and she started sounding off at everyone, getting really touchy and swearing. She knew even more swear words than I do.

She was like that all week but she shut up on Sunday. Her dad was supposed to see her on Sunday. She was sitting waiting for him right after breakfast, though he wasn't supposed to be coming till eleven o'clock. Eleven came and went. And twelve. And then it was lunchtime and Justine wouldn't eat her chicken. She sat at the window all afternoon, not budging.

My tummy went tight whenever I looked at her. I knew what it was like. I used to sit like that. Not just here. I used to wait at both my crummy foster homes. And the children's homes in between. Waiting for my mom to come.

But now I've got myself organized. No more dumb sitting around for me. Because my mom's probably too far away to come on a quick visit. Yeah, that's it, she's probably abroad somewhere, she's always loved traveling.

She's maybe in France.

Or Spain—she likes sunshine.

What am I thinking of? She'll have gone to the States. Maybe Hollywood. My mom looks so great she'd easily get into the movies.

You can't hop on a bus and visit your daughter when you're hundreds and thousands of miles away in Hollywood, now can you?

All the same, even though I don't sit waiting, I always get a bit tingly when there's a knock at the door. I hold my breath, waiting to see who it is, just in case . . .

So I could understand what old Justine was going through. I didn't try to talk to her because I knew she'd snap my head off, but I sort of sidled up to her and dropped a lollipop on her lap and backed away. It wasn't exactly my lollipop. I'd snagged several from little Wayne. His dopey mom is younger than Adele and she hasn't got a clue about babies. Whenever she comes she brings Wayne lollipops. Well, they've got sticks, haven't they? We don't want little Wayne giving himself a poke in the eye. And he normally drools so much that if you add a lot of lollipop-lick as well he gets stickier than superglue. So it's really a kindness to steal his lollipops when he's not looking.

"But why did you want to give one to that Justine?" Louise asked. "She's horrible, Tracy. She barged right into me on the stairs yesterday and she didn't even say she was sorry, she just called me a very rude word indeed." Louise whispered it primly.

"Um. Did she really say that?" I said, giggling. "Oh, she's not so bad, really. And anyway, I didn't give her the *red* lollipop. I saved that for you."

"Thanks, Trace," said Louise, and she beamed at me.

Oh, we were like *that* in those days.

I kept an eye on Justine. She didn't budge for a good half hour, letting the lollipop lie in her lap. And then I saw her hand creep out. She unwrapped it and gave it one small suspicious lick, as if I'd poisoned it. But it must have tasted okay because she took another lick, and then another, and then she settled down for a good long suck. Lollipops can be very soothing to the stomach.

She didn't say thank you or anything. And when she eventually had to give up waiting and go to bed she stalked off by herself. But the next day at breakfast she gave me this little nod. So I nodded back and flicked a cornflake in her direction and she flicked one back, and we ended up having this good game of tiddlyflakes and after that we were friends. Not best friends. Louise was my best friend. Ha.

She moaned at first.

"Why do we have to have that Justine hanging around us all the time?" she complained. "I don't like her, Trace. She's really tough."

"Well, I want to be tough too. You've *got* to be tough. What do you mean? *I'm* tougher than Justine," I said, sticking my chin out.

"You nut job," said Louise.

It started to get to me, though. I started swearing worse than Justine and Jenny got really mad at me because Maxy started copying me and even little Wayne would come out with a real mouthful when he felt like it.

So then I started the Dare Game. I've always won any dare. Until Justine came along.

I dared her to say the rudest word she could think of when the vicar came on a visit. And she did.

She dared me to go out in the garden stark naked. And I did.

I dared her to eat a worm. And she did.

She dared *me* to eat a worm.

I said that wasn't fair. She couldn't copy my dare. Louise opened her big mouth and said I hated worms. "Then I dare her to eat *two* worms," said Justine. So I did.

I *did*. Sort of. It wasn't my fault they made me sick. I did swallow them first. Justine said I just spat them out right away but I *didn't*.

I thought hard. I happen to be a crack hand at skateboarding. Justine's not much good at getting her balance and her steering's rotten. So I fixed up this skateboard assault course around the garden, with sloping benches and all sorts of things. And I dared Justine to take a chance on it. So she did.

She fell over a lot. But she kept getting up and going on. So I said she was disqualified. But Louise

said Justine should still win the bet if she completed the course. And she did.

Then Justine dared me to climb the tree at the end of the garden.

So I did.

It wasn't *my* fault I didn't get all the way to the top. I didn't ask that stupid Mike to interfere. But Justine said I'd lost that dare, and Louise backed her up. I couldn't believe my ears.

Louise was *my* friend.

We couldn't do any more dares because Jenny PUT HER FOOT DOWN. You don't argue when she does that.

The next day Justine's famous dad put in an appearance at long last. Justine had gone on and on about how good-looking he was, just like a pop star, and he actually had an evening job singing in pubs, which was why he couldn't be at home to look after her and her brothers. Well, you should have seen him. Starting to go bald. Pot belly. Medallion on a chain around his neck. He wasn't *quite* wearing a frilly shirt and bell-bottoms, but almost.

You wouldn't catch me wanting a dad like that. But Justine gave a weird little whoop when she saw him and jumped up into his arms like a great big baby. He took her on some dumb outing and when she got back she was all bubbly and bouncy and showing off this . . . this present he'd bought her.

I don't know why, but I felt really annoyed with

← whoops!

Justine. It was all right when she didn't get a visit, like the rest of us. But now I kept picking on her and saying silly sniggery things about her dad. And then she burst into tears.

I was a bit shocked. I didn't say anything *that* bad. And I never thought a really tough girl like Justine would ever cry. *I* don't ever cry, no matter what. I mean, my mom hasn't managed to come and visit me for donkey's years and I don't even *have* a dad, but you won't catch me crying.

And then I got another shock. Because Louise turned on me.

"You are horrid, Tracy," she said. And then she put her arms right around Justine and gave her a big hug. "Don't take any notice of her. She's just jealous."

Me, jealous? Of Justine? Of Justine's dopey dumb dad? She had to be joking.

But it didn't look like she was joking. She and Justine went off together, their arms around each other.

I told myself I didn't care. Although I did care a little bit then. And I did wonder if I'd gone over the top with my remarks. I can have a very cutting tongue.

I thought I'd smooth things over at breakfast. Maybe even tell Justine I hadn't really meant any of it. Not actually apologize, of course, but show her that I was sorry. But it was too late. I was left all alone at breakfast. Louise didn't sit next to me in her usual seat. She went and sat at the table by the window—with Justine.

"Hey, Louise," I called. And then I called again, louder. "Have you gone deaf or something?" I yelled.

But she could hear me all right. She just wasn't talking to me. She wasn't my best friend anymore. She was Justine's.

All I've got is silly squitty twitty Peter Ingham. Oh, maybe he's not so bad. I was writing all this down when there was this tiny tapping at my door. As if some timid little insect was scrabbling away out there. I told this beetle to buzz off because I was busy, but it went on scribble-scrabbling. So eventually I heaved myself off my bed and went to see what it wanted.

"Do you want to play, Tracy?" he said.

"Play?" I said witheringly. "What do you think I am, Peter Ingham? Some kind of baby? I'm busy writing." But I'd been writing so much my whole arm ached and my writing lump was all red and throbbing. Oh, how we writers suffer for our art! It's chronic, it really is.

So I did just wonder if it was time for a little diversion.

"What sort of games do *you* play, then, little Peetle-Beetle?"

He blinked a bit and shuffled backward as if I was about to squash him, but he managed to squeak out something about paper games.

"Paper games?" I said. "Oh, I see. Do we make a football out of paper and then give it a kick so that it blows away? What fun. Or do we make a dear little teddy bear out of paper and give it a big hug and squash it flat? Even better."

Peter giggled nervously. "No, Tracy, pen and paper games. I always used to play tic-tac-toe with my granny."

"Oh, gosh, how incredibly thrilling," I said.

Beetles don't understand sarcasm.

"Good, *I* like tic-tac-toe too," he said, producing a pencil out of his pocket.

There was no deterring him. So we played paper games after that.

I suppose it passed the time a bit. And now I've just spotted something. Right at the bottom of the page, in teeny tiny beetle writing, there's a little message. "I like you a lot, Tracy." Guess what! I've got a letter! Not another soppy little message from Peter. A real private letter that came in the mail, addressed to Ms. Tracy Beaker.

I haven't had many letters recently. Oh, there have been plenty of letters *about* me. Elaine's got a whole library of files on me. I secretly rifled through them and you should just see some of the mean, horrid things they say about me. I had a good mind to sue them for libel. Yeah, that would be great. And I'd get awarded all these damages, hundreds of thousands of pounds, and I'd be able to thumb my nose at Justine and Jenny and Elaine and all the others. I'd just clutch my lovely lollipop in my hot little hand and go off and . . .

Well, I'd have my own house, right? And I'd employ someone to foster me. But because I'd be paying them, *they'd* have to do everything *I* said. I'd order them to make me a whole birthday cake all for

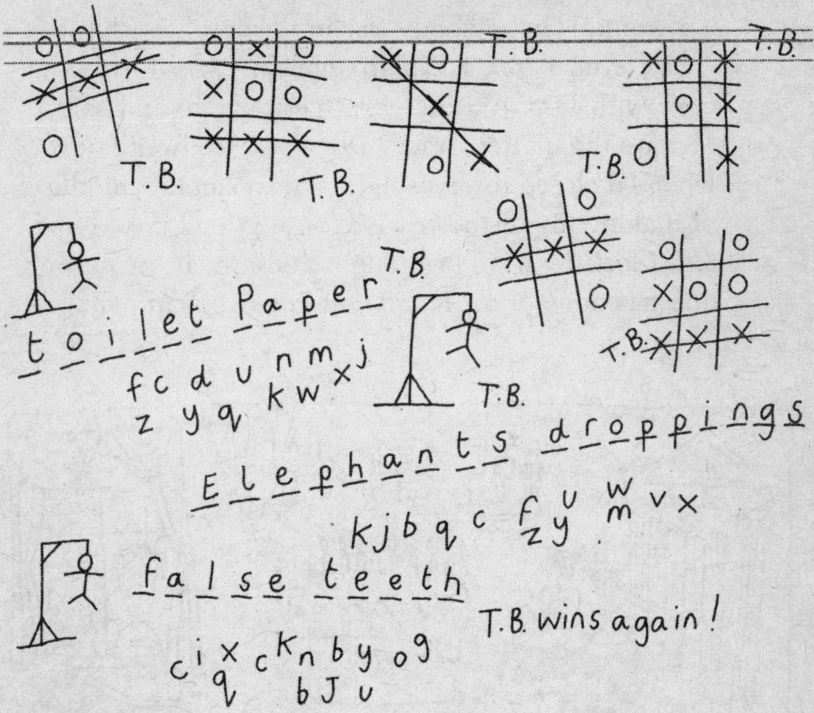

toilet Paper

f c d u n m j
z y q k w x

Elephants droppings

k j b q c f u w
z y m v x

false teeth

c i x c k n b y o g
q b J u

T.B. wins again!

Justine Littlewood's father
met my granny
At the sewage works
he said to her ▓▓▓▓▓▓▓▓ Censored! ↓

I like you
a lot, Tracy.
signed Peter Ingham.

myself every single day of the week and they'd just have to jump to it and do so.

I wouldn't let anybody else in to share it with me.

Not even Peter. I had to share my *real* birthday cake with him. And he gave me a nudge and said, "What's the matter, Tracy? Don't you feel well?" just when I'd closed my eyes tight and was in the middle of making my birthday wish. So it got all mixed up and I lost my train of thought and now if my mom doesn't come for me it's all that Peter Ingham's fault.

Well, maybe it is.

But I'd still let him come over to my house sometimes and we could play paper games. They're quite good fun, really, because I always win.

Who else could I have in my house? I could try and get Camilla. I'd look after her. I could get a special playpen and lots of toys. I've always liked the look of all that baby junk. I don't suppose I had much of that sort of thing when I was a baby. Yeah, I could have a proper nursery in my house and when Camilla wasn't using it I could play around in there, just for a laugh.

I wonder if Camilla remembers me now? That's the trouble with babies.

I wonder if Cam *is* short for Camilla?

That's who my letter was from.

I was a bit disappointed at first. I thought it was from my mom. I know she's never written to me before, but still, when Jenny handed it to me at breakfast I just clutched at the envelope and held it tight and shut my eyes quick because they got suddenly hot and prickly and if I was a snivelly sort of person I might well have cried.

"What's up with Tracy?" the other kids mumbled.

I gave a great swallow and sniff and opened my eyes and said, "Nothing's up! Look, I've got a letter! A letter from—"

"I think it's maybe from Cam Lawson," Jenny said, very quickly indeed.

I caught my breath. "Yeah. Cam Lawson. See that? She's written me my own personal letter. And she's not written to any of you. See! She's written to *me*."

"So what does she say, then?"

"Never you mind. It's *private*."

I went off to read it all by myself. I didn't get around to it for a bit. I was thinking all these dopey things about my mom. And I had a bad attack of hay fever. And I didn't really want to read what Cam Lawson had to say anyway. She saw me having my hairy fit. I was scared she'd think I was some sort of loony.

Only the letter was okay.

So I wrote back to her.

And she wrote back to me.

And I wrote again. And *she* wrote again.

Then she came to see me on Saturday morning. But she really screwed up.

I'd got it all worked out. I was ready to fill her in on all the facts. Mostly about me, of course. But I thought maybe she might fancy interviewing Peter too, to balance things. A girl's point of view, and a boy's. No need to bother with any of the others.

Cam's got this dinky little tape recorder and after just one minute of instruction I mastered the entire mechanism and had great fun fast-forwarding and rewinding and playing back. I took a little turn first, trying out all my different accents, doing my Australian G'day routine and my sinister gangster and my special Donald Duck, but then I decided we'd better get down to business and as I'm not the sort of girl to hog the limelight I said Peter could go first.

He backed away from the tape recorder as if it was a loaded gun.

"Don't be so silly, Peter. Just act normal and speak into it."

"What shall I say?" Peter squeaked.

I sighed impatiently. "Just tell Cam your life story."

"But I haven't got a story. I couldn't think of anything to put when Elaine gave me that book," said Peter. "I lived with my granny. And she died. So I came here. That's all there is."

                                    10 Beech Road
                                    Kingtown

Dear Tracy,

     We didn't really get together properly when
I came on my visit. It was a pity because Jenny
told me a bit about you and I liked the sound of
you. She said you're very naughty and you like
writing.

     I'm exactly the opposite. I've
always been very very good. Especially
when I was at school. You would certainly
have teased me.

     I'm not quite so good now, thank goodness.

     And I hate writing. Because it's what I do for a
living and every day I get up from my cornflakes and go
and sit at my typewriter and my hands clench into fists
and I go cross-eyed staring at the blank paper, and I
think—what a stupid way to earn a living. Why don't I
do something else? Only I'm useless at everything else
so I just have to carry on with my writing.

     Are you carrying on with your writing? You're
telling your own story? An actual autobiography? Most
girls your age wouldn't have much to write about, but
you're lucky in that respect because so many different
things have happened to you.

     Good luck with it.

          Yours,

                    Cam

Dear Ms. Lawson,
           Jenny says that's what I should
call you, Ms. Lawson, although you wrote Cam
at the bottom of your letter. What sort of name is
Cam? If you're called Camilla then I think that's
a lovely name and don't see why you want to muck
it up. I had a friend in this other home called
Camilla and she liked her name. I had a special way
of saying it, Ca-mi i i i-lla, and she'd always
giggle. She was only a baby but very bright.

           Why don't you mind me being naughty?
Actually, it's not always my fault that I get
into trouble. People just pick on me. Lots of
people, but I won't name names because I don't
tell tales, not like _some_ people.

Do you like my drawing? I
liked yours, I thought they
were funny. What do you
mean, you hate writing?

Tracy Beaker did this.
Tracy Beaker did that.
Um, Tracy Beaker is
awful!

GLUE

I think that's weird when it's what you do. I like writing. I think it's ever so easy. I just start and it goes on and on. The only trouble is that it hurts your hand and you get a big lump on your finger. And ink all over your hand and clothes and paper if some clueless toddler has been chewing on your felt-tip pen. Are you having trouble writing your article about us? I could help you if you like. I can tell you anything you need to know about me. And the others. How about it?

Yes, I am still writing my autobiography. I like that word. I asked Jenny and she said it's a story about yourself, and that's right, that's exactly what I'm writing. I'd let you have a look at it but it's strictly personal. Don't take any notice of what that moron Justine read. There are some really good parts, honest.

Yours,
From your fellow writer
Tracy Beaker

R.S.V.P.
That means you've got to reply.

10 Beech Road

Dear Tracy,

Thanks for your lovely letter. It made me laugh. Do you know what? I think you're a born writer.

I could do with some help on my feature.

Are you around next Saturday morning? Hope to see you then. Cam.

I hate Camilla. I used to get teased rotten at school for having such a soppy name.

Dear Camilla,
        It's not a soppy name. You've got to be proud of it. You want to try having a name like Tracy Beaker. Excuse this crummy writing paper. Jenny lent me the first batch but she says I'm costing her a small fortune in paper and can't I give it a rest. So I borrowed this from one of the little ones. Isn't it yucky? I know.

← This is Goblinda the Goblin and she's going to gob all over these dumb fairies.

Yes, I'll help you out on Saturday. If I'm there, of course.

My Mom often comes to take me out. Although she may be abroad just now. I think she's going to take me on a trip abroad too. But it mightn't be for a while, so I'll see you on Saturday morning probably. About what time? We have breakfast at 8:30 on Saturdays and I always eat quickly so about 8:35?

Yours, from your fellow - hang on, I'm not a fellow

Yours, from another lady writer,

Tracy

R.S.V.P.

So I know what time to start waiting.

10 Beech Road

Dear Sister Writer,

See you Saturday morning. 8:35 impossible.

I look like this at 8:35.

How about 10:35?

Cam. Sorry. Camilla. Ugh!

P.S. I love Goblinda. Put her in a story.

"That's okay, Peter. Don't let Tracy bully you into it. You don't have to say anything," said Cam.

"What a nerve! I'm not a bully. Huh, *I* was the kid who always *got* bullied. This other Home I was in, there was this great big teenage guy, and he was a really tough skinhead and he had these stomper boots and I filled them up with custard for a joke and he didn't see the funny side of it but he looked really hilarious, all this frothy yellow liquid squishing up his trouser legs—so anyway, from then on my name was mud, and he really had it in for me. The things he used to do!"

I was about to launch into a long account but—typical typical—that Justine Littlewood came barging over.

"It's not fair, Ms. Lawson. You're letting that stupid Tracy show off like mad, and you're not giving any of us a turn."

"You shut your face, blabbermouth," I said. "She hasn't come to see you. She's come to see *me*. A strictly private appointment. So get out of here. Isn't that right, Cam?"

"Well. Yes, I've come to talk to you, Tracy. But we

could all take a turn on the tape recorder for a bit," she said.

What a gutless creep she is! She was there just to see *me*. We had a proper business appointment. All she had to do was tell Justine and the others to buzz off. It wouldn't have mattered if Peter stayed, because he's not really any bother. But the others! It was useless. Practically the whole morning was wasted. She let them all mess around on the tape recorder and then some of the little kids wanted another turn drawing with her Mickey Mouse pen, and then Jenny came in with coffee for Cam and soda for us and it was like some big party. Only I didn't feel like the birthday girl. I felt squeezed out to the edge again.

After a bit I stomped off. I kept looking back over my shoulder and I thought she didn't even notice. But then she sidled up. She still had baby Becky on one hip and little Wayne clinging to her leg like a limpet. She gave me a dig in the back with her Mickey Mouse pen.

"Hey," she said softly. "Shall we get started on your interview now, Tracy?"

"Well, you've got all these other kids. Why waste your time with me?" I said acidly. "I mean, I'm only the one you were *supposed* to see."

"Tell you what. Let's go up to your room. Just you and me. How about it?"

"Okay," I said, yawning and shrugging. "If you really want. I'm not interested in the idea now. But if you insist. Just for a minute or two."

It took her a while to dump the baby and pry
Wayne away, and then all the others kept cluster-
ing around, saying it wasn't fair. So do you know
what she did? She said they could do interviews on
her tape recorder. And she put *Justine* in charge
of it.

"You sure are making a mistake there, Cam.
You're crazy. They'll wreck it in two minutes," I
said.

"No they won't. Justine will work it. And everyone
take a two-minute turn. Introduce yourselves first,
and then say whatever you want. But don't worry,
Peter, you don't have to."

"You are stark staring mad," I said. "Look, if anyone's in charge of that tape recorder it's got to be

me. I'm the only one who knows how to work it properly."

"Well, show Justine," said Cam. "Then she'll be able to work it too."

"I'm not showing *her*," I said. But in the end I did. And of course Justine was clueless and didn't catch on and I kept sighing and groaning and she got upset and gave me a push and I clenched my fist ready to punch her, but Cam got in between us and said, "Look, I'll run through it. Here's the Record button, Justine, right?" and *eventually* Justine got the hang of it. I don't know why she's called Littlewood. Little*brain* would be far more appropriate.

Then Cam and I went up to my room and left them to it.

"You thought you'd found a way of getting Justine

THIS ROOM BELONGS TO
TRACY BEAKER
STRICTLY PRIVATE
KEEP OUT ON PAIN OF DEATH.
AND IT WILL BE A VERY PAINFUL
DEATH TOO.

and me to make friends," I said. "But, ha-ha, it didn't work, did it? Because we're always going to be deadly enemies."

Cam laughed at me. She laughed at the notice taped on my bedroom door too.

"It's okay. You can come in. You're my guest," I said, opening the door for her.

My room looked like a rubbish dump, actually. I hadn't got around to making the bed and the floor was littered with socks and pajama tops and bits of cookie and pencil sharpenings, so she had to pick her way through. She didn't make a big thing of it, though. She looked at all the stuff I've got pinned to my bulletin board, and she nodded a bit and smiled.

"Is that your mom?" Cam asked.

"Isn't she lovely? You'd really think she was a movie star, wouldn't you? I think she maybe *is* a movie star now. In Hollywood. And she'll be jetting over to see me soon. Maybe she'll take me back with her, and I'll get to be a movie star too. A child star. The marvelous movie moppet, Tracy Beaker. Yeah. That would be great, eh?"

I spun around with a huge grin, doing a cutesie-pie curtsy. Cam caught on right away and started clapping and acting like an adoring fan.

"I hope you're still going to be a writer too," she said. "Have you done any more about Goblinda?"

"Give me a chance. I've been too busy doing my autobiography," I said.

"I suppose this autobiography of yours is strictly private?" Cam asked, sounding a bit wistful.

"Of course it is," I said. But then I hesitated. Elaine the Pain has seen bits of it. And Louise and Littlebrain. And I did show a bit to Peter, actually, just to show him how much I'd done. So why shouldn't I show a bit to Cam too? As she's sort of a friend.

So I let her have a few peeks. I had to be a bit careful, because some of the stuff I've written about her isn't exactly flattering. She came across a description of her by accident, but she didn't take offense. She roared with laughter.

"You really should be the one writing this article about children in foster care, Tracy, not me. I think you'd do a far better job of it."

"Yes, have you made a start on this article yet?"

She fidgeted a bit. "Not really. It's difficult. You see, this magazine editor wants a very touching sentimental story about all these sad sweet vulnerable little children that will make her readers reach for a wad of Kleenex."

"Yeah, that's the right approach."

"Oh, come off it, Tracy. None of you are at all *sweet*. You're all gutsy and feisty and spirited. I want to write what you're really like, but it won't be the sort of thing the editor wants."

"And it won't be the sort of thing *I* want either. You've got to make me sound sweet, Cam! No one will want me otherwise. I've gone past my sell-by date already. It gets hopeless when you get older than five or six. You've stopped being a cute little toddler and started to be difficult. And I'm not pretty either, so people won't take one look at my photo and start cooing. And then it's not like I'm up for adoption, so people can't ever make me their little girl, not properly."

"You're not up for adoption because you've still got your mom?"

"Exactly. And like I said, she'll be coming for me soon, but meanwhile I'd like to live in a proper homey home instead of this old dump. Otherwise I'll get institutionalized."

Cam's eyebrows went up.

"I know what it means and all. I've heard Elaine and some of the other social workers going on about it. It's when you get so used to living in an institution like this that you never learn how to live in a proper home. And when you get to be eighteen you can't cope and you don't know how to do your own shopping or cooking or anything. Although I can't see me ever having that problem. I bet I could cope right this minute living on my own. They'd just have to hand me the money and I'd whiz off down the shops and have a whale of a time."

"I bet you would," said Cam.

Then Maxy started scratching at my door and whining and complaining. I told him to go away, because Cam and I were In Conference, but he didn't take any notice.

"Ms. Lawson, it's not fair, them big girls won't let me have a turn on the tape, I want a turn, you tell them to let me have a turn, they're playing they're pop stars, and *I* want a turn."

Cam smiled and sighed, looking at her watch.

"I'd better go back downstairs. I've got to be going in a minute anyway."

"Oh, that's not fair! Aren't you staying? You can have lunch with us, Jenny won't mind, and it's hamburgers on Saturday."

"No, I'm meeting someone for lunch in town."

"Oh. Where are you going, then?"

"Well, we'll probably have a drink and then we'll have a salad or something. My friend worries about her figure."

"Who wants boring old salad? If I was having lunch out I'd go to McDonald's. I'd have a Big Mac and french fries and a strawberry milk shake. See, I'm not the slightest bit institutionalized, am I?"

"You've been to McDonald's, then?"

"Oh, lots of times," I said. And then I paused. "Well, not actually *inside*. I was fostered with this boring family, Julie and Ted, and I nagged them to take me, but they said it was junk food. And I said all their boring brown beans and soggy veggie stews were the *real* junk because they looked like someone had already eaten them and upchucked them and— well, anyway, they never took me."

"No wonder," said Cam, grinning.

"I am allowed to go out to lunch from here, you know."

"Are you?"

"Yes. Any day. And tell you what, I really will work on that article for you. I could work on it this week and show you what I've done. And we could discuss it. Over lunch. At McDonald's. Hint, hint, hint."

Cam smacked the side of her head as if a great thought has just occurred to her.

"Hey, Tracy! Would you like to come out with me to McDonald's next week?"

"Yes, please!" I paused. "Really? You're not kidding?"

"Really. Next Saturday. I'll come and pick you up about twelve, okay?"

"I'll be waiting."

And I will. I'd better send her a letter too, just in case she forgets. I know she said twelve o'clock. And she's not exactly the most punctual of people.

The dumping ground.

Dear Camilla,

I'm working hard on the article. I'll show you on Saturday. Remember we have a lunch-date. At 12. To go to McDonald's.

From your co-writer Tracy Beaker.

P.S Goblinda says if you took her to McDonald's she'd be ever so good and wouldn't gob once.

She might not get here till ten past. Even twenty or half past. So why am I sitting here staring out the window when we've only just had breakfast?

I hate waiting. It really gets on my nerves. I can't concentrate on anything. Not even my writing. And I haven't done any writing in this book all week because I've been so busy with my article for Cam. I've got it all finished now and even if I do say so myself I've done a really great job. She can just hand it to her editor and no one will be any the wiser. I should really get the whole fee for it myself. But I'm very generous. I'll share fifty-fifty with Cam, because she's my friend.

Old Pete's my friend too. We've been bumping into each other in the middle of the night this week, on a sheet sortie. Mostly we just whispered a little, but last night I found him all huddled up and soggy because he'd had a nightmare about his granny. Strangely enough, I'd had a nightmare about my mom and it had brought on a bad attack of my hay fever. Normally I like to keep to myself at such moments since some stupid ignorant twits think my red eyes and runny nose are because I've been crying. And I never *ever* cry, no matter what.

But I knew Peter wouldn't tease me so I huddled down beside him for a bit and when I felt him shivering I put my arm around him and told him he was quite possibly my best friend ever.

He's just come up to me now and asked if I want to play paper games. Yeah, it might pass the time.

_ A _ I L L A   L A _ _ O N

B K   U D E Y J P   T R Y

Oh, charming! Peter and I had just got started and I was about to win the first game when Elaine the Pain comes buzzing in. She's here dumping off some boring new kid and now she wants to have a little chat with Peter.

"Well, tough, Elaine, because *I'm* having a little chat with Peter right now," I said.

"Now now, Tracy," said Elaine.

"Yes, *now*," I said.

Elaine bared her teeth at me. That smile means she'd really like to give me a smack in the head but she's going to make allowances for me.

"I expect you're feeling a bit het up this morning, Tracy, because of this writer coming to take you out. Jenny's told me all about it. It'll be a lovely treat for you."

"You bet. And it'll be a lovely treat for her too because I've written this article for her."

"Well, I might have a little treat up my sleeve for Peter here," Elaine said, and she shuffled him off into a corner and started talking to him earnestly.

She's still talking to him. She's keeping her voice down. But I can have very large waggly ears when I want. Elaine's going on about these people she knows. An older couple whose children have all grown up. And now they're a bit lonely. They'd like to look after someone. A little boy. Maybe a little boy just like Peter.

So that's it. Little Peetie-Weetie is obviously going to get fostered and live Happily Ever After.

Well, that's good, isn't it? Because he's my best friend.

No, it's bad, because he won't be able to be my best friend anymore if he goes off and gets himself fostered.

And it's not fair. He's hardly been here any time. I've been here ages and ages and no one ever wants to foster me now.

Still, who wants to be fostered by some boring older couple anyway? Older might mean really ancient. And crabby. And strict. They'd never wear jeans or write funny letters or take Peter to McDonald's.

I wish Cam would hurry up and come for me. Although it's nowhere near time. It's stupid sitting here by the window like this. Waiting.

Justine is hovering behind me. I think she's waiting for her dad. I hope she won't tell him about the little accident with her Mickey Mouse clock. He might come and beat me up. Even though the clock's all mended now. Jenny took it into this shop and they fixed it. I was glad to see old Mickey ticktocking around and around again. Justine caught me looking and she gave me this big hard push that nearly knocked me over and told me that if I so much as touched her clock again she'd beat me up good and proper. Honestly! My fists clenched and I was all set to give it to her because no one talks to Tracy Beaker like that, but then I remembered my lunch date. Jenny isn't best pleased with me at the moment. If I got into a fistfight with Justine then she might not let me go out with Cam.

So I Kept Calm. I smiled at Justine in a superior sort of way.

"Really, Justine, do you always have to resort to violence?" I said.

My superior willpower was wasted on Justine. She just thought I was chicken.

"Cowardy cowardy custard," she was mumbling under her breath now. "Tracy Beaker's got no guts."

I'm not going to take any notice of her. I'll just sit here writing. And waiting. It's not *that* long now. Only it seems like forever.

I used to sit like this. When I waited for my mom. I wonder when she will come. I had that awful dream about her. I was out having lunch with Cam in McDonald's and it was really great and we were

having a fabulous time together when I looked up at the clock and saw it was past one o'clock, and it suddenly rang a terrible bell in my head, and I remembered that my mom was coming to take me to lunch at one o'clock, and I just went panic panic panic.

I charged off to try to get back to the Home in time and I got a bus but they threw me off because I didn't have enough money and then I ran into Auntie Peggy and she chased after me to give me a

good smacking and Julie and Ted tripped me and
Justine caught me and threw me in a river and I
couldn't swim and I was drowning . . . and then I
woke up. Wet.

So okay, I know it was only a dopey old nightmare. But what if it was some kind of *premoni-
tion*??? What if my mom really comes for me today
and I miss her because I'm having lunch with Cam?
I'll have to talk to Elaine.

Well, I've talked. Sort of.
"Can I have a little chat, Elaine?" I said.
"Tracy. I'm still having a little chat with Peter."
"You've *had* a little chat with Peter. Correction.
You've had an extremely long and boring endless con-
versation with him. And you're my social worker just
as much as his. So could you *please* come and have a
little chat with me? It's sort of urgent."
Elaine sighed. She ruffled Peter's hair and gave
him a little chuck under the chin. Then she came
over to me at long last.

"What is it then, Tracy?"

I swallowed, not sure how to put it.

"Tracy, are you just playing with me?" said Elaine.

"No! It's just . . . Look, about my mom. She doesn't know I'm here, does she?"

"Well. No, I don't think so."

"But if she wanted to find me she could, couldn't she?"

I said it in a whisper but Justine heard.

"Who'd ever want to come looking for you, Tracy Beaker?" she said.

"You shut your mouth!"

Justine made a hideous face and Louise giggled. Then she tugged at Justine's sleeve.

"Come on. Let's see what that new girl's doing. She's got two whole suitcases with her, so she must have heaps of clothes."

But Justine wanted to stay at the window so Louise wandered off by herself. I knew Justine was still listening for all she was worth (honestly, some people have no decency whatsoever) but I had to keep on asking Elaine.

"If my mom wanted she could go to that old children's home. And they could tell her where I am now, couldn't they?"

"Yes, of course they would," said Elaine. "Don't worry, Tracy. Each time you get moved somewhere else, there's a special record kept. So if your mom wants to see you it's easy. They look up your name and file number and find your present address."

"Good," I said.

"What's up, Tracy? You still look a bit worried."

"I'm okay."

Only I don't feel okay. What if my mom does come today? And I'm out having lunch with someone else? Will she wait for me? Or will she get fidgety and fed up and zoom off again? And I'll get back here and Jenny will say, "Oh, by the way, Tracy, your mom called when you were out, but she couldn't wait for you. She was all set to take you back to Hollywood with her but she had this plane to catch so she couldn't hang around."

What am I going to do?

Maybe she won't come today. She hasn't ever come before. And yet, what if she did? I *wish* I hadn't had that dream. Dreams *can* come true.

I feel sick. Maybe I don't really want to go to McDonald's after all.

See that? It's real blood.

I'm not going to get to go to McDonald's now, whether I want to or not. I've had a fight. I'm in the Quiet Room.

This is how it happened. I went over to Peter. I whispered in his ear.

"Would you like to go to McDonald's with Cam?"

Peter scrunched up his neck because my whispers can be a bit tickly.

"You mean, go with you?"

"No. Go instead of me. I've kind of lost interest in the idea. It's okay, I'll tell Cam when she comes. She likes you a lot, so she won't mind taking you instead."

Peter looked worried.

"I can't, Tracy. I'm going out too. With these people."

"What, with this boring older couple?" I said.

Elaine raised her eyebrows at me but I took no notice.

"I bet they won't take you to McDonald's," I said.

"Why don't *you* want to go, Tracy?" Elaine asked. "I thought you were so looking forward to it."

"Yes, but . . . I want to stay here. Just in case."

Elaine is a pain but she's also quite quick at putting two and two together.

"Tracy, I don't think your mom will be coming today," she said quietly.

"Oh. I know that. Only I had this dream. She did in the dream."

"Yes, I'm sure she did. And I expect it was a lovely dream, but—"

"No, it was a perfectly foul dream because I wasn't here to see her and—"

"And you woke up blubbing with a soaking wet bed, *baby*," Justine muttered.

"I told you to shut *up*," I said, getting really riled.

"I'd go out with your writer friend, Tracy," said Elaine.

"Mmm. Well. I'm not sure I really want to now,

115

anyway." I glare at Peter. "Why do you have to be seeing this boring old couple today, eh? You could see them any old time. You go and have a Big Mac with Cam."

Peter wriggled. Elaine put her hand on his shoulder. He looked up at her and then at me.

"Sorry, Tracy. I want to meet them. Auntie Vi and Uncle Stanley."

"Of course you want to meet them, Peter. And Tracy is going to meet her writer," said Elaine.

"No, I'm not."

"*I'd* go," said Justine. "Only I can't, because of my dad. I'm going out to lunch with him."

"You were supposed to be going out with him last Saturday. Only he never turned up," I said.

"Okay, but he does come *sometimes*. Not like your famous mom. She's never ever ever come for you," said Justine.

"Oh yes she has!" I yelled. "She's come for me lots of times. She's going to come and take me away for good, we're going to Hollywood together and—will you stop *laughing* at me, you great big pig."

"You're so stupid," Justine gasped. "Your mom's not a movie star. Louise told me about your mom. She's nothing. And she's never coming for you. She hasn't been near you since you were little. I bet she's forgotten all about you. Or she's had heaps of other kids and doesn't want to think about that boring ugly Tracy ever again."

So I hit her. And I kept on hitting her. And I don't care. I've made her nose bleed again. She's hurt me a bit too, but I don't care. And now I'm stuck in the Quiet Room and it's past twelve and one of the other kids will get to go out to lunch with Cam instead of me and I don't care. At least it won't be Justine.

Maybe my mom *will* come.

There's someone outside the door. It's opening. *Is it Mom???*

No. It wasn't Mom. It never is. It was Cam, of course.

I took one look at Cam and burst into tears. Well, I would have, if I was a crying sort of person.

"Oh dear," said Cam. "I don't seem to have a very good effect on you, Tracy."

She sat right down on the floor beside me, waiting for me to quiet down a bit. Then she dug in the pocket of her jeans and found a crumpled tissue. She passed it to me and I mopped up my hay fever.

"Now," said Cam. "What do you want to do?"

"I haven't got any choice, have I? I'm stuck here."

"No you're not. You can still come out to lunch with me. I've asked Jenny. Elaine explained why you got upset."

"She doesn't know! I hate the idea of everyone all blabbing away about me," I said fiercely.

"Yes, it must get a bit annoying," said Cam. "Still, at least it means you're the center of everyone's attention. Here, you've still got a runny nose. Good thing you weren't wearing your makeup this time."

"Are you laughing at me?"

"Just a little tease. Coming?"

"You bet."

Only I *still* felt bothered about my mom, even though I knew it was silly. I knew she almost definitely wouldn't be coming. I knew deep deep down that Justine was maybe right about her. But I still worried.

"My mom," I mumbled.

"You're scared she'll come and you won't be here?" said Cam. "Okay. Tell you what we'll do. You can phone home when we're out. To see if she's arrived. And if she *has* I'll whisk you straight back. How about that?"

"That sounds great," I said.

So Cam and I went off together for our lunch appointment after all. She's got this ancient grass-green Citroën, which was a bit of a change from the minivan.

"My mom wouldn't be seen dead in this sort of icky car," I said. "She drives a Cadillac, you know."

"Mmm," said Cam.

I squinted at her. "You're just nodding to be nice to me, aren't you?" I said. "You don't really believe my mom's got her own Cadillac."

Cam looked at me. "Do you believe it, Tracy?"

I thought for a bit. "Sometimes."

Cam nodded again.

"And sometimes I know I'm sort of making it up," I mumbled. "Do you mind that? Me telling lies?"

"I make things up all the time when I write stories. I don't mind a bit," said Cam.

"I've got that article with me. I've written it all. You won't have to bother with a thing. Shall I read a bit to you? You'll be really impressed, I bet you will. I think I've done a totally professional job."

So I started reading it to her.

" 'You can see the signs of suffering on little Tracy Beaker's elfin face. This very very intelligent and extremely pretty little girl has been grievously treated when in so-called care. Her lovely talented young mother had to put her in a children's home through no fault of her own, and in fact she might soon be coming for her lovely little daughter, but until then dear little Tracy Beaker needs a foster family. She is deprived and abused in the dump of a children's home'—Why are you laughing, Cam?"

"Abused?" Cam spluttered.

"Look at my hand. My knuckles. That's blood, you know."

"Yes, and you got it bouncing your fist up and down on poor Justine's nose," said Cam. "You're the one who deprives and abuses all the others in your Home."

"Yes, but if I put that no one will want me, will they?"

"I don't know," said Cam. "If I were choosing, I'd maybe go for a really naughty girl. It might be fun."

I looked at her. And went on looking at her. And my brain started going tick tick tick.

I was mildly distracted when we got to McDonald's. I ate a Big Mac and a large portion of french fries, and washed it down with a strawberry milk shake. So did Cam. Then she had coffee and I had another milk shake. And then we sat back, stuffed. We both had to undo our belts a bit.

I got out my article again and showed her some more, but she got the giggles all over again.

"I'll give myself hiccups," she said weakly. "It's no use, Tracy. I think it's great, but they'll never print it. You can't say those sorts of things."

"What, that Tracy Beaker is brilliant and the best child ever? It's true!"

"Maybe! But you can't say all the other things, about Justine and Louise and the rest."

"But they're true too."

"No, they're not true at all. I've met them. I like

them. And you certainly can't say those things about Jenny and Mike and your social worker and all the others. You'd get sued for libel."

"Well, you do better then," I said huffily. "What would you put?"

"I don't know. Maybe I don't want to do the article now anyway. I think I'd sooner stick to my stories and forget about the money."

"That's not a very professional approach," I said sternly. "Maybe you ought to give up writing. Maybe you ought to do some job that gives you a big fat allowance. Looking after someone. You get an allowance for that."

Cam raised her eyebrows.

"I can barely look after myself," she said.

"Well, then. You need someone to look after you for a bit," I said. "Someone like me."

"Tracy." Cam looked me straight in the eye. "No. Sorry. *I* can't foster you."

"Yes you can."

"Stop it. We can't start this. I'm not in any position to foster you."

"Yes you are. You don't need to be married, you know. Single women can foster kids easy-peasy."

"I'm single and I want to stay single. No husband. And *no kids*."

"Good. I hate other kids. Especially boring little babies. You won't ever want to have a baby, will you, Cam?"

"No fear. Holding that little Wayne was enough

122

to douse any maternal urges for all time," said Cam.

"So it could be just you and me."

"No!"

"Think about it."

Cam laughed. "You are *so* persistent, girl! Okay, okay, I'll think about it. That's all. Right?"

"Right," I say, and I tap her hand triumphantly. "Can I phone home now? I sound like E.T., don't I? We've gone through two videos of that already. So, can T.B. phone home? Only she doesn't have any change."

Cam gave me ten pence and I went to the phone by the rest room and gave Jenny a buzz. My heart did thump a bit when I was waiting for her to answer. I felt a little bit sad when she told me that Mom hadn't come. Even though that was the answer I was really expecting.

But I had other things to fuss about now. I whizzed back to Cam.

"Well? Have you thought about it? Is it okay? Will you take me on?" I asked eagerly.

"Hey, hey! I've got to think about this for ages and ages. And then I'm almost certain it's still going to be no."

"*Almost* certain. But not absolutely one hundred percent."

"Mmm. What about you? Are you absolutely one hundred percent sure you'd like me to foster you?"

"Well, I'd sooner you were rich. And posh and all that, so that I could get on in the world."

"I think you'll get on in the world without my help, Tracy."

"No, I need you, Cam."

I looked straight at her. And she looked straight at me.

"We still hardly know each other," she said.

"Well, if we lived together we would get to know each other, wouldn't we, Cam? Camilla. That sounds classier. I want my foster mom to sound absolutely classy."

"Oh, Tracy, give it a rest. Me, classy? And I told you, I can't abide Camilla. I used to get teased. And that's what my mom always called me." She made a face.

I was shocked by her tone and her expression.

"Don't you . . . don't you *like* your mom?" I said.

"Not much."

"Why? Did she beat you up or something?"

"No! No, she just bossed me around. And my father too. They tried to make me just like them, and when I wanted to be different they couldn't accept it."

"So don't you see them anymore?"

"Not really. Just at Christmas."

"Good, so they'll give me Christmas presents, won't they, if I'm their foster grandchild?"

"Tracy! Look, it really wouldn't work. It wouldn't work for heaps of practical reasons, let alone anything else. I haven't got room for you. I live in this tiny apartment."

"I'm quite small. I don't take up much space."

"But my apartment's really minute, you should see it."

"Oh, great! Can we go there now?"

"I didn't mean—" Cam began, but she laughed again. "Okay, we'll go to my apartment. Only I told Jenny I'd take you back to the Home after lunch."

"T.B. can phone home again, can't she?"

"I suppose so. Tell Jenny I'll get you back by dinnertime."

"Can't I come to dinner with you too? Please?"

"Tell you what. We could pretend to be posh ladies just to please you and have afternoon tea. About four. Although I don't know how either of us could possibly eat another thing. And then I'll take you back to the Home by five. Right?"

"What about dinner? And look, I could stay the night, we're allowed to do that, and I don't need pajamas, I could sleep in my underwear, and I needn't bother about washing things, I often don't wash back at the Home—"

"Great! Well, if you ever lived with me—and I said *if*, Tracy—then you'd wash all right. Now don't carry on. Five. Back at the Home. That'll be quite enough for today."

I decided to give in. I sometimes sense I can only push so far.

I phoned, and Cam spoke to Jenny for a bit too.

"T.B.'s phoned home twice now. Like E.T. Do you know what E.T. got?" I said hopefully. "Smarties."

"You'll be in the Sunday papers tomorrow, Tracy.

125

THE GIRL WHOSE STOMACH EXPLODED," said Cam.

But she bought me Smarties all the same. Not a little tube, a great big packet.

"Wow! Thanks," I said, diving in.

"They're not just for you. Take them back and share them with all the others."

"Oh! I don't want to waste them."

"You're to share them, greedyguts."

"I don't mind sharing them with Peter. Or Maxy. Or the babies."

"Share them with everybody. Including Justine."

"Hmm!"

She stopped off at another shop too. A bakery. She made me wait outside. She came out carrying a cardboard box.

"Is that cakes for our tea?"

"Maybe."

"Yum yum. I'm going to like living with you, Cam."

"Stop it, now. Look, Tracy, I seem to have got a bit carried away. I like seeing you and I hope we can go out some other Saturdays—"

"Great! To McDonald's? Is that a promise?"

"That really is a promise. But about fostering . . . I'd hate you to build your hopes up, Tracy. Let's drop the subject now and just be friends, okay?"

"You could be my friend *and* my foster mom."

"You're like a little dog with a bone. You just won't let go, will you?"

"Woof woof!"

I'm getting good at making her laugh. I like her. Quite a lot. Not as much as my mom, of course. But she'll do, until my mom comes to get me.

Her apartment came as a bit of a shock, mind you. It really is weeny. And ever so shabby. It's in a far worse state than the Home. And you should see her bedroom. She leaves her pajamas on the floor too!

Still, once I get to live there I'll get her organized. Help her make a few improvements.

"Show me your books then," I said, going over to the shelves. "Did you write all this?"

"No, no! Just the ones on the bottom shelf. I don't think you'll find them very exciting, Tracy."

She was absolutely right about that. I flicked through one, but I couldn't find any pictures, or any funny bits, or even any rude bits. I'll have to get her to write some better books or she'll never make enough money to keep me in the style to which I want to become accustomed.

Maybe I'll have to hurry up and get my own writing published. I got Cam to give me a good long turn on her typewriter.

It took me a while to get the hang of it. But eventually I managed to tap out a proper letter. I left it tucked away on Cam's desk for her to find later.

```
     DEAR  CAM,  I  WILL  BE  THE  BESTEST  FOSTER
CHILD  EVER.  YOU'LL  SEE.  WITH  LOVE  FROM  TRACY
BEAKER,  THE  GIRL  WHOSE  STOMACH  DIDN'T  EXPLODE.
```

It nearly did, though. Guess what she bought for tea! A birthday cake, quite a big one, with jam and cream inside. The top was just plain white, but she took some of my Smarties and spelled out T.B. on the top.

"So that it's all my cake," I said happily.

"Aren't I going to get a slice?" asked Cam.

"Oh, yes. Of course. But I don't have to share it with anyone else. I had to share my proper birthday cake with Peter, wasn't that *mean*!"

"I thought Peter was your friend."

"Well. He is. But still. You don't want to share your birthday cake, even with your bestest friend ever," I said.

Only I started thinking about it all the time I was chomping my way through my first great big slice. And my second slice with extra jam and cream. And my third weeny slice. And my nibbles at a bit of icing.

"This is much better than that birthday cake at the Home, you know," I said.

"Good."

"Peter's gone out with this dumb-sounding old auntie and uncle today," I said.

"Has he?"

"But I bet they won't take him to McDonald's. Or buy him his own special cake."

"Maybe not."

"Well, seeing as we are friends, Peter and me, and we share a birthday, and we shared that other birthday cake—maybe we *ought* to share this one too," I said. "Shall I take a slice back for my friend Peter?"

"I think that would be a good idea," said Cam. "I'll wrap up a slice for Peter. And another slice for you. Just so long as you promise me you won't throw up all night."

"Of course I won't. Here, can I do the cutting this time? Because if this is like a birthday cake I get a wish, don't I?"

So Cam gave me the knife and I closed my eyes and wished really really hard.

"I bet you can't guess what I wished," I said to Cam.

"I bet I can," said Cam.

"I'll tell you if you like."

"Oh no. You're supposed to keep birthday cake wishes secret," said Cam.

I made a little face at her. Then I thought.

"Here, if this is a sort of birthday, then it's a pity there aren't any presents too." I paused. "Hint hint hint."

"Do you know what you are, Tracy Beaker? Absolutely shameless."

But it worked!

Cam looked all around her room and stared for a while at her bookshelves. I thought I was going to end up with a boring old book. But it was much much better. She went to her desk and picked up her Mickey Mouse pen.

"Here we are, Tracy. Happy Unbirthday," she said, and she pressed the pen into my hand.

Just for a moment I was lost for words. And that doesn't happen very often to me. I was scared I might even get another attack of my hay fever. But I managed to grin and give her the thumbs-up sign and show her that I was ever so pleased.

We got back to the Home at five. On the dot. Trust her to be punctual at the wrong time. I made a bit of a fuss on the doorstep. I sort of clung a bit. It was just that I was enjoying myself so much that I wanted to go *on* enjoying myself. That's not being difficult, is it?

But it's still okay. She's coming next Saturday. She's promised. Twelve o'clock. We have a date, me

and my future foster mom. I'm going to make that wish come true.

It took me a bit of time to calm down after we'd said goodbye. I missed out on dinner, but it didn't really matter, seeing as I'd had more than half my cake and the McDonald's lunch and the Smarties. There were still quite a few Smarties left. Just no red ones. Or pink or mauve or blue. They're my favorite colors. But there were plenty of the boring ones to share with the others.

When I came out of the Quiet Room I collected my Smarties and the two slices of cake. They'd got a bit squashed as I was saying goodbye to Cam, but Jenny helped me spruce them up a bit and put them on a plate.

I went to find Peter. He was up in his room, sitting on his bed, looking a bit quiet.

"Uh-oh," I said. "This older couple. They didn't turn up?"

"Oh yes. They did," said Peter.

"But they were pretty awful, yes? Never you mind, Pete, see what I've got for us? Look, really yummy cake."

"Thank you, Tracy," said Peter, and he took his slice absentmindedly. "No, they aren't awful, Auntie Vi and Uncle Stanley. They're nice, actually."

"I bet they didn't take you to McDonald's."

"No, we went and had fish and chips. My granny and I always used to go and have fish and chips. With bread and butter and a cup of tea."

"Boring! I had a Big Mac and french fries and a strawberry milk shake, two actually, and then Cam bought me these Smarties and then she bought me this really incredible cake and even put my initials on the top. It was my extra special cake and I could have eaten it all up myself but I asked her to save a big slice for you. So I did. And you haven't even started on it yet. Don't you like it? It was meant to be your big treat."

"Oh, it's lovely, Tracy," said Peter, munching politely. "It's ever so good of you. I told Auntie Vi and Uncle Stanley all about you and said you were my best friend. They want to meet you very much."

"Well, it's no use them getting interested in me. I'm going to be fostered by Cam, you wait and see."

"Really? That's wonderful. You see, I think Auntie Vi and Uncle Stanley want to foster me, Tracy. That's what they said. They want to take me almost right away."

"So you're zooming off and leaving me in this dump, are you?" I said. "Terrific!"

"Well. I don't *want* to leave you, Tracy. I told them that. But if you're going to be fostered too . . ."

"Yeah, yeah, well, Cam's desperate to have me, but you shouldn't always rush into these things, you know, Peter. You should think it over carefully."

"I know. That's what I've been trying to do," said Peter. "Tracy. No matter who fosters me, who fosters you, we can still stay best friends, can't we? And visit each other lots? And write letters?"

"I'll write you letters with my very own special Mickey Mouse pen. Want to see it?"

"Oh, Tracy, you didn't steal it from Cam, did you?"

"Hey! What do you take me for? She gave it to me, dumbo. I told you she's crazy about me. Okay, we'll make a pact. We'll stay best friends no matter what. Here, you're leaving all the icing. Don't you like it?"

"Well, I was saving the best bit till last. But you have it, Tracy. I want you to have it, really."

It's quite good, sharing a cake with your best friend. Then I went around the whole Home with the packet

of Smarties. I gave one
each to everyone. I even
gave one to Louise and the
new girl. They were up-
stairs together, trying on
the new girl's clothes.

Justine was down-
stairs. At the window.
Her dad hadn't turned
up. She had a new Band-
Aid on her face. She was sniffling.

I looked at her. My heart started going thump
thump thump. I went up to her. She turned around,
looking all hopeful. She thought I was Louise. But it
looks like Louise might have a new best friend now.
Louise is like that.

Justine jumped a bit when she saw it was me.

"What do you want, Tracy Beaker?" she mumbled, wiping her eyes.

"I've got something for you, Justine," I said.

I thought I was going to give her a Smartie. But you'll never guess what I did. I gave her my Mickey Mouse pen.

I must be stark staring bonkers. I hope Cam can get me another one. Next Saturday. When I see her. When she tells me that she's thought it all over and she wants to be my foster mom.

This started like a fairy tale. And it's going to finish like one too. Happily Ever After.

Jacqueline Wilson has written more than seventy books for young readers of all ages. In England, her *Double Act* won both the Children's Book of the Year Award and the Smarties Prize. Jacqueline Wilson also won the Children's Book Award for *The Suitcase Kid*, *The Illustrated Mum*, and *Girls in Tears* and has been short-listed five times and runner-up twice for the prestigious Carnegie Medal.

Jacqueline Wilson lives near London in a small house crammed with fifteen thousand books.